THE WIDE-AWAKE
princess

THE WIDE-AWAKE
princess

E. D. BAKER

SCHOLASTIC INC.
New York Toronto London Auckland
Sydney Mexico City New Delhi Hong Kong

ISBN 978-0-545-32845-6

12 11 10 9 8 7   16/0

Printed in the U.S.A.   40

First Scholastic printing, January 2011

Book design by Donna Mark

This book is dedicated to my fans, whose loyalty and enthusiasm has meant so much to me—particularly the fans on my message board, those who send letters, and those who send their wonderful entries to my contests. It is also dedicated to my family, whose understanding about late dinners and a messy house enables me to keep writing.

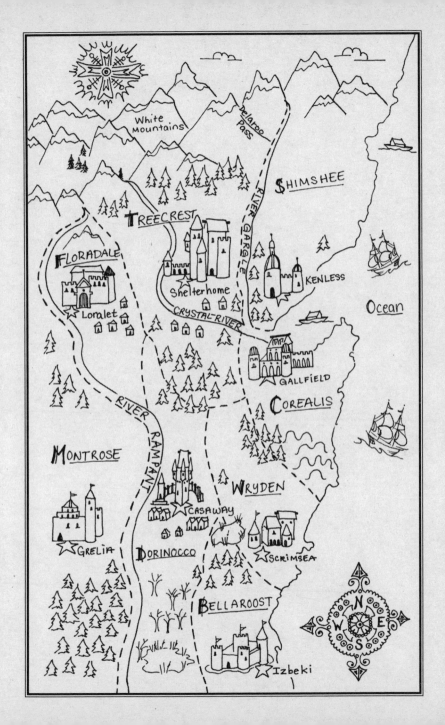

THE WIDE-AWAKE
princess

PROLOGUE

"WE CAN'T LET IT HAPPEN again," Queen Karolina said, dabbing at the tears that glistened in her deep blue eyes. "A wicked fairy casting a horrid spell on my firstborn child was almost more than I could bear. Halbert and I have been frantic with worry ever since, and our poor little Gwendolyn has suffered so much. She can't even visit her grandparents because they refuse to banish spinning wheels from their kingdom."

"Tsk, tsk," said the fairy Moonbeam, shaking her head in dismay.

"I banished all the spinning wheels from Treecrest the day after Gwendolyn's christening," said King Halbert.

The infant stirred in the queen's arms. Queen Karolina glanced down at her sleeping daughter, then back to the fairy dressed all in silver. "I don't know what I'd do if that nasty fairy were to curse my sweet Annabelle, too. It's time we planned my little darling's christening, but we wanted to consult with you first."

"We were hoping you might be able to suggest something, Moonbeam," said the king. "You are Karolina's favorite fairy godmother. Even in Treecrest, the Fairy of the Moonflower Glade is known as the wisest of all the fairies."

Moonbeam pursed her lips as she tucked a lock of her silvery hair back in place. She tapped her chin as she thought, then nodded and said, "I have a suggestion, but you aren't going to like it."

Queen Karolina glanced at her husband as another tear trickled down her flawless cheek. When the king nodded, his wife turned back to her fairy godmother. "It can't be worse than living in fear that our little girl is going to prick her finger and sleep for a hundred years. Whatever it is, we'll do it!"

"So be it," said Moonbeam, taking her magic wand out of a purse made of moonbeams and cobwebs. "Your daughter shall receive only one magical gift, and it shall be mine." As the parents held their breath, the fairy raised her magic wand and tapped the sleeping infant on the forehead. "From this day on, no magic shall touch you or bring you to harm. You'll have to survive on your natural charm."

Sparkling fairy dust sprinkled down onto the little princess. The baby sneezed, opened her eyes, and began to wail.

"What did you mean about surviving on her natural charm?" the king shouted over his daughter's squalling.

"Neither good nor bad magic can ever touch her now," the fairy replied as she tucked her wand back into her purse. "She's going to grow up a normal girl, without magic to make her beautiful or graceful or sweet."

Bending over the baby, the fairy kissed her forehead where the wand had touched her, then vanished in a puff of silver sparkles. The baby scrunched her tiny pink face and screamed until she turned red as a beet.

The queen's hands began to shake. She glanced down and discovered that a freckle had appeared on the back of one of her own fingers. The king noticed it as well and gestured for the nanny to take the baby away.

"Oh, Halbert, what have we done?" asked the queen.

"I'm afraid, my dear," the king replied, "that we might have just made a very big mistake."

CHAPTER 1

IT WAS PRINCESS GWENDOLYN'S sixteenth birthday and everyone was frantic. It wasn't that they weren't ready for the celebration; the kitchen had been in an uproar for days as the cooks prepared all of Gwendolyn's favorite foods, the floors had been scrubbed and strewn with fresh herbs, and every inch of the Great Hall had been cleaned and decorated until it was almost unrecognizable. Everyone was agitated because it was the last day left for the curse placed on Gwendolyn to come true.

The people of Treecrest lived in dread that their beautiful princess might still touch a spinning wheel. They had taken precautions and had searched every room twice a week ever since the fairy announced the curse. Although spinning wheels had been banished, one never knew when a nasty witch or evil fairy could plant one in a room, just waiting for the princess to come along and start poking things she shouldn't. Early that morning the guards had begun to search the entire castle once again.

Princess Annie, Gwendolyn's younger sister, offered to accompany the guards, just as she did at least once a week. They'd start with the old tower in the north end of the castle. It had been abandoned years before and had fallen into disrepair, but it was on the inspection list because it was exactly the kind of place that evil people liked.

They had started at the top of the tower and were working their way down. The top two floors held only three rooms each, but the floors below them were riddled with small rooms, which made searching them that much slower. In order to speed it up, the guards divided themselves into smaller groups. Annie went with Horace, an older man with gray hair and a short beard, and Liam, a new recruit who had come to the castle the week before.

Like her sister, Gwendolyn, Annie was petite. Liam was only a few years older than Annie and taller than most boys his age; the top of Annie's head came up only to the middle of his chest. Annie liked his shaggy, dark hair and his deep blue eyes, and she thought that his quick smile made him instantly likable. The only things that kept him from being too handsome were his slightly crooked teeth and a dimple in one cheek but not the other. As far as Annie was concerned, they were the very things that made him more attractive.

Normally, Annie wasn't impressed by a handsome man, because nearly all whom she'd met had been made that way by magic. Liam was different, however. Although his glance was respectful and nothing more, it was distracting to have him there, and she had to force herself to think about the reason she had gone to the tower.

While the guards shoved doors open and peered around corners, Annie wandered through the rooms, paying more attention to what she heard than what she saw. She was walking along the corridor when she heard a faint sound like pieces of metal clanging together a long way off. Although magic couldn't touch her, she could sense its presence. The strength and type of magic determined how it sounded; the stronger the magic, the louder it was, and the good kind didn't sound anything like the bad.

Annie followed the sound, trying to pinpoint where the magic was strongest. There, behind the door with the cracked frame. Annie knew that the door opened onto a room that was too small to be of much use—but big enough to fit a spinning wheel.

When Horace started toward her, Annie shook her head. "Stay back. I'll let you know if I need you."

"What is it?" asked Liam as he came up behind her.

"Nothing I can't handle," she replied. She could hear the older guard murmuring to him, but their voices were drowned out when she placed her hands on the cracked wood and the clanging metal sound grew louder in her

6

head. Annie shoved the door open and discovered an old woman sitting before a spinning wheel inside the tiny room, her fingers moving with expert skill as she spun a long silver thread.

"Welcome, my dear," the old woman croaked, turning just enough that Annie could see her wrinkled cheek and the glint of an eye beneath the concealing cape and hood. "Come in and see what I'm making just for you. See how the thread shines? Go ahead and touch it. Feel how soft it is."

"You have got to be joking!" said Annie. "I'm not touching that thing!"

The old woman turned toward her, letting her hood fall away. Her wrinkled face was contorted in an angry scowl as she pointed one of her gnarled fingers at Annie and said, "You're not Princess Gwendolyn! You're not even beautiful. Why, I have rats in my poison pit that are prettier than you!"

"I'm not Gwendolyn," said Annie. "And you're an evil old hag."

"You little whelp! Talk to me that way, will you? Just for that, I'm going to turn you into a beetle and squash you where you stand!" Reaching into the depths of her cloak, she pulled out a slender stick and aimed it at Annie.

"I wouldn't do that if I were you," Annie warned. She stuck her fingers in her ears to block the sound of clanging that she knew was about to get louder.

Eyes flashing, the old woman muttered something

under her breath. The air around the tip of the stick glowed and crackled. A bolt of light shot out of the stick, hit an invisible wall in front of Annie, and hurtled back the way it had come, knocking the old woman off the stool.

"No!" screamed the old woman as her hands scrabbled at her chest. "This isn't supposed to happen! What did you—" Her voice turned into a moan as her body shrank and her skin hardened into the carapace of a beetle. Her hair seemed to get sucked into her head as her face grew pinched and narrow.

Annie thought it was revolting, but she couldn't make herself look away until the two guards edged past her and into the room.

"What happened here?" asked Liam as a normal-looking beetle scuttled across the floor.

"She turned herself into a beetle," said Annie. "Be careful where you step," she told Horace, who was walking around the spinning wheel. There was a loud crunch and he stopped to look down.

"I guess I found her," Horace said, inspecting the bottom of his shoe.

Annie swallowed and looked away. She thought she should probably feel sorry for what had happened, but she hadn't hurt the woman herself. That bug had been a human just a minute ago and had planned the same fate for her.

Liam grabbed the spinning wheel and began to lug it

8

toward the door. It was bigger than the opening, however, so he turned to Horace, who was busy scraping the goop off his shoe.

Horace grunted, and together the two guards hauled the spinning wheel into a bigger room. "We should probably keep searching the tower," said Annie, following them. "That woman's magic sounded like a witch's, not a fairy's, although I don't know why a witch would come when a fairy cast the curse. Maybe the fairy is still coming."

Liam looked from Annie to Horace, a puzzled expression on his face.

"Our princess can tell when magic is around," Horace said, sounding proud. "There's not many that can do that."

"It is an unusual skill," said Liam, "and most useful."

Annie noticed the look in his eyes, more interested now and not just respectful.

"You go with the other men, Your Highness," said Horace. "Liam and me are going to break this up and burn it." He jabbed his thumb in the direction of a fireplace in the back of the room.

Annie joined another pair of guards and stayed with them while they finished inspecting the tower and the rooms below it. She knew she should go see her sister, who was probably still unwrapping presents, but she wanted to avoid having to listen to her go on and on about Prince Digby, the man Gwendolyn would probably marry.

9

Her parents both said that Gwendolyn and Digby were suited for each other. The magic of his own fairy godmothers had made him as handsome as Gwendolyn was beautiful. But Annie was convinced that by concentrating on his appearance, the fairies had forgotten a few very important qualities: Digby had as much intelligence as a block of stone and an equal amount of compassion for others. Annie didn't like him, and he didn't like Annie.

Digby did like beautiful people, and while Annie was many things, she knew that she was hardly beautiful. Her bottom lip was a little too full and her brown eyes weren't striking like Gwendolyn's violet ones. Although Gwendolyn's silken locks were a glorious buttercup yellow, Annie's tangled curls would have been a muddy brown if she hadn't spent so much time outside, where the sun bleached them yellow white like a goat girl's.

Annie knew that there was another even more important reason why her parents wanted Gwendolyn to marry Digby. He was from the wealthy and militarily strong kingdom of Shimshee, to the east. The marriage would create an alliance between the two kingdoms, benefiting Treecrest, which had been made poor by years without spinning wheels. Of course, King Halbert was already planning to bring spinning wheels back into the kingdom after Gwendolyn's birthday, whereupon they could once again make the yarn and hence the cloth from the fiber of the linder tree, the most valuable natural resource located within the kingdom's boundaries. Even so, it would be years before Treecrest could call itself wealthy again.

Thinking about Digby put her in a sour mood, so when the guards spread out into the rest of the castle, Annie decided that she needed to be by herself. *At least Digby isn't here*, she thought, relieved that she wouldn't be running into him in the hallways. For many years, guests had been discouraged from coming for fear of one smuggling a spinning wheel in with their luggage. Unlike most princes, who expected a formal invitation, Digby had come to visit the first time uninvited and unwelcome. After they got to know him, her parents thought he was harmless, and then he visited all too often. Annie had been delighted when Digby's father had summoned him home shortly before Gwennie's birthday.

Even without guests, so many people lived in the castle that it was always full. Knowing that the garden was usually empty in the morning, however, Annie was taking a shortcut through the Great Hall when the singing began. She groaned, having forgotten the minstrels for the few hours she'd been upstairs.

Minstrels of every description had been flocking to the castle for the last week, planning to sing at Gwendolyn's birthday celebration. They had been allowed in provided they carried nothing but their instruments, which they immediately began practicing every day.

There were so many of them now that it was hard to find a quiet place in the public areas of the castle. All the minstrels had written their own songs praising "the most beautiful princess in the world." Annie thought that any sane person would consider them pests and want to hide in a trunk until they went away, but Gwendolyn would probably bask in their songs and wonder why there weren't more of them.

Blocking out the voices wasn't easy. "Your beauty is like a summer's day, remembered in the winter," began one song. She smiled and nodded as she passed the minstrel leaning against the wall, trying to avoid meeting his eyes. If they made eye contact, politeness would dictate that she stop and listen, and being polite was the last thing she felt like doing just then.

Another minstrel was seated in front of the servants who were hanging the last of the flower garlands. "You smile at everyone you see, when all your smiles should be for me," the minstrel sang. Annie grimaced, and had almost made it to the door when a poet who had arrived the day before stepped in front of her. "Would Your Highness like to hear my latest poem?" he asked, moving to block her as she tried to walk around him. "I'd love to hear what you think of it."

"No, thank you," said Annie. "I have urgent business I must attend to." Although lying made her uncomfortable, she thought that listening to fools was worse.

"This won't take but a minute," the young man said.

Raising his hand in the air, he struck a pose and began, "I saw you first just yesterday, sweet Gwendolyn, divine…"

"I really do have to go," Annie said, edging past him.

The poet scowled, brightening when he saw that a group of people had come up behind her. "And thought your face perfection…," he continued as Annie slipped through the door.

The garden had been created in what had once been an otherwise empty area between the keep, the curtain wall, and two outbuildings. In a space where pounded earth and stone had been all there was to see, flowers now grew in abundance regardless of the time of year. A gift from the fairies of Floradale, Queen Karolina's home kingdom, the flowers in the garden never faded. If cut, the stems regrew overnight and bloomed again by morning.

In coming to the garden, Annie had hoped to find a quiet place to think, but there was no quiet in the garden that day. Gardeners carrying woven baskets snipped flowers for bouquets, talking among themselves as they moved from plant to plant. Three young men had been given the special chore of stripping the rosebushes of their blossoms; roses were Gwendolyn's favorite flower.

Unable to stay in the garden, Annie climbed the nearest set of narrow stairs to the battlements. With the castle grounds on one side of her and the outside world on the other, there was always plenty to see. The Crystal River flowed along the western side of the castle, making a natural barrier against attack. A moat dotted with water lilies bordered the castle on the other three sides, thereby surrounding it with water. There were two drawbridges, but only one opened to a road that led into the town of Shelterhome. The other drawbridge set down on a road that led across open fields to the woods, and it was in that direction that Annie was looking when the cart came into sight.

Because most carts were driven directly to the town of Shelterhome, seeing one headed for the castle was enough to make Annie pause. The cart itself didn't look like much; it was a typical farm cart with two horses pulling it and a man perched on the seat. The only thing on the back of the cart was a large trunk, its metal hasps shining in the sunlight. Annie watched with interest as the cart approached the drawbridge and waited for the guards to let it pass. She could hear the wheels rumbling across the wooden planks. In less than a minute they were clattering over stone.

Annie turned around to watch it enter the courtyard, where it trundled toward a row of carts that had come from town. The driver added his cart to the end of the row, then pulled his hat low over his eyes and seemed to fall asleep. Now that it was closer she could see that the cart wasn't exactly like the ones in front of it; the back of the seat was curved instead of straight, and there were curious markings on the side, as if someone had tried to paint over an emblem using too-thin paint.

One by one, the contents of the carts were

inspected before servants hauled the goods into the castle. Because of Gwendolyn's birthday, there were more carts than usual, and many of their burdens were gifts for the princess. Even so, each was inspected, including the gifts that had been wrapped. Containers big enough to hold a spinning wheel were given special attention.

Growing bored, Annie moved on until she was able to look out over the Crystal River. She loved Treecrest and wouldn't have minded spending the rest of her life there, but thinking about Gwendolyn's marriage made her wonder about her own future. Normally, princesses were expected to marry handsome princes who would ride up on fiery stallions and carry the loves of their lives off to their own magnificent castles, where they would, of course, live happily ever after. Those were normal princesses, however, made perfect through a fairy god-mother's magic, not ordinary girls with ordinary talents. Girls who hadn't been given magic gifts were considered less than desirable. No prince had ever shown the slightest interest in marrying Annie.

For the last three centuries, the few princesses in their family who had never married remained at home, living with their parents, and later with whatever sibling inherited the throne. Everyone knew that Gwendolyn would marry soon after her sixteenth birthday. As the older daughter in a family without sons, whomever she married would join her on the throne someday. If

Gwendolyn married Digby, Annie was convinced that he would hate the idea of having her live with them.

The shriek of a hawk made Annie look toward the woods, where the strange cart she'd seen arrive was trundling back to the forest, moving faster now that it was free of its load. Reaching the edge of the woods, the driver jumped down and another man emerged from among the trees to take his place. Annie thought this was very odd, and even odder still when three men climbed down from the trees and clapped him on the back as if he'd done something special.

When the men melted into the forest, Annie headed for the stairs. There was something not quite right about what she'd just seen, so she wanted to talk to the captain of the guards. He looked up at her approach.

"Thank you for your help this morning, Your Highness," said the captain. "If you hadn't been there, the witch would have turned my men into beetles. I know my men. They would have made lousy beetles."

"You're quite welcome, Captain. I'm glad I was able to help. But there's something that you might want to look into now. I saw a man who delivered a trunk here take his cart into the forest. Another man changed places with him and he went into the woods on foot."

"It's odd, but nothing criminal," said the captain. "Perhaps someone else was going to take the cart back so the man you saw could visit friends in Shelterhome. Did you hear anything unusual when you saw him?"

"No, there was nothing."

"Then it must be all right," the captain said, his expression lightening. "Magic would have been the biggest threat. And no one tried to slip any spinning wheels past us in the gifts today. I'm sure there's nothing to worry about."

"Thank you, Captain," Annie replied. "I'm probably worrying more than I should."

"It was your worrying that saved us this morning," said the captain. "And everyone's grateful for that."

CHAPTER 2

ANNIE NODDED TO THE MESSENGER and hurried up the stairs to the queen's chamber. Ordinarily she would have been surprised and delighted to be summoned to her mother's rooms, but this time she knew why her mother wanted her, and it wasn't to thank Annie for finding the witch.

Annie almost never entered her mother's rooms. It wasn't by choice, however. In accepting the fairy Moonbeam's gift, the king and queen had unwittingly accepted a second "gift" on Annie's behalf. The same spell that prevented magic from touching her worked as a damper on other people's magic. Should anyone be close to Annie for any length of time, whatever magic gifts they had been given began to fade, whether it was beauty, charm, or something as simple as the ability to unravel even the most difficult knots. Gwendolyn hadn't been the only member of the family to be given magical gifts at a christening. Both the king and queen had as many magical attributes as their elder daughter. On the rare occasion that Annie entered the chamber of one of her family members, she was expected to sit in the back as far from them as she could without climbing out the window. The same was true of the Great Hall when everyone assembled for meals; Annie had to sit in the opposite end of the room with the daughters of lesser nobles, none of whom had much magic.

More than anything, Annie wanted to feel as if she belonged. But instead she felt as if she were a remote and not-too-fondly regarded cousin who was allowed to live in the castle. Although she'd tried very hard to please her parents, nothing their ordinary daughter could do had ever been enough to earn her the same affection that they showered on Gwendolyn.

Annie sighed, and knocked on the door. When one of her mother's ladies-in-waiting let her in, Annie found her mother waiting for her in a chair by the fireplace. Although she was over forty years old, the queen looked as young as her daughters. The only time she showed her age was when Annie came near, which the queen was careful to avoid.

"I want you to go straight to your sister's chamber," said Queen Karolina. "I've heard that you spent the morning looking for spinning wheels, when the guards are

19

quite capable of doing it without you. Today is Gwendolyn's birthday. The least you can do is sit with her while she opens the rest of her presents."

"But I'll have to sit in the back of the room and I won't see a thing when everyone stands up."

"I'll be there and I'll make sure they stay seated. Your sister wants you there today and so do I. We don't do enough together as a family."

"Will Father be there, too?" asked Annie. She saw her father even less than she saw her mother and sister, and looked forward to talking to him.

Queen Karolina appeared puzzled. "Why would he be? He hates this kind of thing. We'll see him during the jousting and races this afternoon. You'll sit on the other side of the field, of course, but we'll all be there. Now go attend your sister. You know I do everything I can to make you feel included. It isn't as though I ask very much of you."

"Of course not, Mother," said Annie. She would have liked to have kissed her mother's cheek as she'd seen Gwendolyn do, but she knew it wasn't allowed. Even the mention of it would make her mother angry, not at Annie, but at the situation, as the queen told anyone who would listen. Annie was the one she would take it out on, however, lecturing her on being considerate of others and how awful it would be for the kingdom if she, the queen, were to lose her beauty.

Once she was dismissed, Annie bowed to her mother

and escaped from the room. She still didn't want to go to Gwendolyn's chamber, however, and when she arrived, the first thing she said was, "Maybe I shouldn't stay. I don't want to make you look less than your best on your birthday."

"Pish posh!" said Gwendolyn. "Just sit in the back like you always do and nothing bad will happen."

Annie glanced at the ladies-in-waiting. She could tell by the expressions on their faces that they didn't want her in the room any more than she wanted to be there. The daughters of high-ranking nobles, they each had been given magically enhanced qualities like beauty and charm, although none of them were as beautiful as Gwendolyn.

"We were just admiring the gowns Prince Digby sent me," said Gwendolyn as Annie made her way to a chair by the back wall.

The ladies-in-waiting watched her go, their expressions turning to one of approval when she finally sat down. Annie knew that they would be friendly, as long as she didn't get too close.

"He sent twenty gowns of the finest linder cloth!" announced Lady Cecily, the youngest of Gwendolyn's attendants. She held up a gown of violet trimmed in silver. "Isn't this lovely!"

"It certainly is," said Annie. "The color matches your eyes, Gwennie."

Gwendolyn blushed, her perfect cheeks turning a

lovely shade of pale rose. "I've asked you not to call me that. It doesn't sound very regal."

"Neither does Annie, and you've called me that my whole life," Annie replied, and turned to look out the window. She didn't want to see her sister pout or let tears gather in her eyes or any of the other ploys Gwendolyn used to get her own way.

"There you are, my dear," said Queen Karolina from the doorway. "I'm delighted to see that you decided to join your sister while she opened her presents."

Annie sighed and turned away from the window. If her mother wanted everyone to think that Annie had come there voluntarily, that was her business. "Good morning, Mother," she said, getting to her feet just as everyone else had already done.

"Please be seated," the queen said, taking the chair closest to Gwendolyn, causing the young woman who had been sitting there to find another seat. "This is an informal gathering, after all."

Gwendolyn sat with her hands in her lap while the ladies-in-waiting changed seats, vying for the best place to see what she had received. Everyone knew that once the princess tired of a gift, she gave it to whoever had admired it the most. Over the years her ladies had received some beautiful trinkets that way.

Once everyone was settled in their seats, Gwendolyn clapped her hands, saying, "I have a special treat for you."

At her nod, Cecily ran to open the door, admitting a

stream of servants bearing trays. One of the princess's christening gifts had been a perfect figure, so she could eat anything she wanted to without gaining weight. Her favorite foods were sugary pastries and delicate finger foods, most of which were too rich for Annie. While the beautiful ladies with the perfect figures wolfed down one pastry after another, Annie nibbled the edges of the one she'd taken just to be polite. It was so sweet that it made her teeth hurt, but she smiled and tried to look as if she was enjoying it. After a few minutes her stomach started to gurgle; for once she was glad she was seated by herself.

Gwendolyn began to open her next present. Although the kingdom's treasury was low, gifts had been arriving from every corner of Treecrest as well as most of the neighboring kingdoms. When the ladies surrounding her tried to stand up to get a better look, Queen Karolina ordered them to sit down, then turned toward Annie and smiled. Even so, Annie couldn't see the gifts very well. She didn't really pay attention while Gwendolyn held up jewelry and more gowns. However, when servants brought in the trunk she had seen delivered earlier that day, Annie finally stood. It was a distinctive trunk with etched metal hasps and she wondered who had sent it.

The ladies drew closer as Gwendolyn opened the trunk and reached inside to take out a piece of parchment, which she discarded without reading. Annie craned her neck, trying to see. There was a collective gasp as her sister lifted out a miniature tree about a foot tall. The tree was so delicately carved that even from a distance Annie was sure it had to be the work of an elf-trained master woodworker. She took an involuntary step toward the front of the room when the branches shivered and parted, revealing a jeweled bird no bigger than her fist. When her sister began to turn a key attached to the bird's back, Annie drew closer. No one noticed, however, because they were all engrossed in watching the bird flutter its wings and tilt its dainty head. Annie held her breath when it opened its beak and began to warble a tune so sweet that some of the ladies-in-waiting wiped tears from their eyes.

The moment the bird stopped singing, the ladies burst into applause. They were still clapping when a seam appeared in the bird's side, splitting it in two and revealing a small egg of an especially lustrous gold.

"Oh!" everyone breathed, including Annie. She wondered for a moment if it was magical, but decided it wasn't when she didn't hear anything that made her think of magic.

Gwendolyn turned the tree around, revealing another, smaller key at the base of the egg. Beaming with delight, she wound the key, which made the egg spin and play a merry tune that soon had the ladies tapping their feet. This time when it stopped, the sides split in quarters, revealing a tiny object covered with precious gems.

"What is it?" said Gwendolyn.

The sides of the egg continued to lower. When they were down all the way, the object tilted to one side and tumbled out of the egg.

Gwendolyn's hand shot out and caught the object before it hit the floor. "I have it! Look! It's lovely. What do you think it is? Oh!" she exclaimed, looking at her hand in dismay.

"No, it can't be!" cried the queen, who had been leaning forward to see the object better.

Annie gasped at the sound of tinkling wind chimes that only she could hear. The air suddenly seemed denser. All the color in the room faded and sounds became muffled; only the faint dinging of the wind chimes remained. Although all the other ladies looked as if they were moving through thick soup, Annie could still run. She was nearly there when Gwendolyn's eyes drifted shut and she slumped in her chair. A moment later, the queen, who had started to stand, fell to the floor as limp as a rag doll, while the other ladies collapsed around her.

Somewhere in the castle, something crashed and shattered, but the sound was muffled and Annie couldn't tell its direction. "Help!" she yelled to the guards. "Come quickly!" But there were no answering footsteps. The only sounds that Annie could hear were the soft snoring of the sleeping women and the continued tinkling of wind chimes.

The long-ingrained habit of not touching members

of her family was difficult to break, but Gwendolyn had become so pale that Annie was afraid. Taking her sister's wrist in her hand, Annie breathed a sigh of relief when she felt a strong, steady pulse. A hint of color returned to Gwendolyn's cheeks, making Annie think that there might be reason to hope that it wasn't as bad as it seemed.

Gwendolyn stirred, her eyelids opening a crack. "What happened?" she asked, her words slurred.

"I'm not sure," said Annie. She glanced at the jeweled object still held in her sister's hand. Although Gwendolyn hadn't recognized it, Annie knew what it was right away. Someone had crafted a tiny model of a spinning wheel only an inch tall, yet perfect in every detail, right down to the tiny spindle, where a drop of Gwendolyn's blood quivered.

"It was a spinning wheel," Annie explained. "Someone sent it here to make the curse put you to sleep. It looks as if it's put everyone else to sleep, too."

"That's nice," Gwendolyn murmured, her eyelids sagging.

"No, it's not!" said Annie. "It's terrible. Do you think you can stand?"

"Course I can stand," Gwendolyn grumbled when Annie shook her. "I have grace and poise, unlike some people." Opening one eye, she gave Annie a baleful glare. "Poor little Annie. You never were graceful. I could always dance circles around you. Maybe I will later, when I'm not so tired." Gwendolyn opened her mouth wide in an unladylike yawn. Her two front teeth were crooked now. Being so close to her sister was already taking its toll.

Annie pulled Gwendolyn's arm across her shoulders and hauled her to her feet. "You'll have to help me if I'm going to get you to your bed," said Annie. "Put one foot in front of the other ... That's right."

"I always have had to help you, haven't I, Annie?" said Gwendolyn as she dragged her other foot forward. "No magic, that's your problem. Always felt sorry for you. Told Digby, 'I don't care if she's homely, she's still my sister.'"

Annie jerked her forward a little harder than she needed to and said, "You're too kind."

While Gwendolyn stumbled along, yawning mightily, Annie half dragged, half carried her into the next room. Gwendolyn's movements were no longer so graceful and she looked awkward when she tried to climb onto the high bed. She couldn't quite make it to the mattress, so Annie had to give her a shove. The older sister sprawled across the bed with an *oof!* and flopped over onto her back.

"That's better," Gwendolyn murmured as she stretched out her legs. Annie stepped back. The moment she let go of her sister, the color drained from Gwendolyn's face again, but her teeth straightened themselves.

"I should check on the others," said Annie. She had heard her mother snoring, so she knew she was all right, but she wasn't so sure about the rest of the castle's inhabitants. There had been that crashing sound, after all. Someone might have been hurt when the curse took hold.

Annie nearly tripped over a sleeping guard when she stepped into the corridor. It was littered with bodies and looked at first as though there had been a battle in which everyone had died without shedding a drop of blood. She started down the corridor and was relieved to find that they were all sleeping. A few people looked as if they were sleeping peacefully slumped against the wall, but there were others who Annie was certain must be uncomfortable with their bodies twisted at odd angles and their heads canted to one side. She helped the worst of these, touching them long enough to get them in more comfortable positions. They woke for the short time she touched them, but they were so drowsy that not one of them questioned her.

Just down the corridor from Gwendolyn's room, Annie found a serving girl stretched atop the shards of a shattered pitcher, snoring. "This must have been what crashed," Annie muttered, and made sure that the girl hadn't cut herself. She continued on and was amazed that no one had gotten hurt, not even the scullery maid who had fallen asleep with her sleeve in the fireplace. It was almost as if the fire had gone to sleep as well, for it seemed to be just a shadow of flames and not hot enough to burn. Even so, she moved the girl away from the fireplace and doused the fire with a pot of soup cooling on the table. It barely fizzled when it went out.

Annie was crossing the Great Hall when she realized that over the unceasing sound of the wind chimes she could hear the faint tap of her soft-soled shoes hitting the herb-covered floor. It was a sound she had never heard before, at least not in the Great Hall. The Hall was the heart of the castle and normally bustling with activity at all hours of the day and night. The sounds of people talking, dogs barking, pages playing games, and, lately, the music of the minstrels had made it one of the liveliest places in the castle. She had never heard it so quiet before, and it made her stop and listen. The people were still there, of course, draped across the tables and sprawled on the floor where they'd landed when they collapsed. Some of them were even snoring, but the faint sound was lost in the huge room, and for the first time that day, Annie began to feel afraid.

She walked more quickly now, still hoping that she might find someone awake. When she discovered her father sitting upright on the oversized chair in his private meeting room, she thought for a second that he might not have fallen prey to the curse, but as she approached she realized that he, too, was asleep and that the wide curving back of the chair was all that kept him from falling over like the nobles around him. Annie left him there, unable to help him any more than she could her mother or sister.

She was walking through yet another corridor when she glanced out the window and an idea occurred to her. Retracing her steps, she entered the Great Hall and looked for one of the little dogs that some of the ladies of the court always kept with them. She found one at the feet of an old lady she'd never really liked. She hadn't liked the dog, either, but he was small and easy to carry, so she picked him up, petting his head to calm him when he came partially awake.

Stepping around the sleeping guards at the door, Annie crossed the courtyard and reached the drawbridge. It was still down, but with no one to guard it she wondered how long it would be before someone who had no right to be there wandered in. The little dog seemed perkier now that they were outside, and Annie began to think that her plan might really succeed. Maybe the curse worked only as long as its victims were inside the castle. Maybe she could bring them out and everyone would wake up.

Thinking that the soft tinkling music she heard was part of the magic in the castle, Annie ignored it when she knelt to lay the little dog on the ground. "Ow!" she exclaimed, scrambling to her feet. Prickly rosebushes had started sprouting from the normally soft grass and she nearly stumbled over one that had sprung up behind her. Retreating to the road that led to the drawbridge, she set the dog near the edge of the moat. Although the dog had been alert enough to lick her hand just moments before, as soon as she was no longer touching him the little animal's eyes shut and he went limp, making breathy sounds as if he had inhaled too much dust.

"So much for that theory," Annie muttered as she

scooped up the little dog. Cradling him in her arms, she recrossed the drawbridge, returning to the courtyard within the castle walls as the climbing roses twined around the taut cables. She stopped once she was past the portcullis and looked back. The roses had already covered the drawbridge, but didn't seem to be growing past the walls. Instead, they twisted and looped around themselves, reaching higher than her head and creating an impenetrable barrier armed with long, razorlike thorns.

Annie shuddered and hugged the little dog tighter, disliking the roses even though they weren't a bad idea. Everyone in the castle was sound asleep and likely to stay that way for years, if she remembered the curse correctly, which meant that whoever had made the roses grow around the castle wall had probably done it to keep people out rather than in. Even so, a wall like this would protect her family and friends better than any guards. Unfortunately, it also meant that Annie was trapped, or would have been if she hadn't known a secret or two about the castle.

Annie had no intention of staying in the castle. If she did, she'd be long dead before anyone in her family woke up. There had to be something she could do to end the curse, but she'd have to leave the castle to find whatever it was. Her family should be fine where they were until she got back, which wouldn't be long if she was lucky.

Hurrying to the Great Hall, she paused before stepping inside. Although she was used to the faint music of

31

the wind chimes and was able to block them out, there was something different, or at least she hadn't noticed it before. Everyone was just as she had left them, and their breathing was just as deep and regular, but now it was more uniform. All the people seemed to be inhaling at the same time, and exhaling in unison. The noise was faint, but it almost sounded as if the castle was breathing. It frightened her enough that she tiptoed across the stone floor, positioned the dog beside his owner as quietly as she could, and tiptoed out again.

Annie crept up the stairs, on edge now in a way she hadn't been before. The sound of breathing wasn't as obvious in the stairwell as it was in the Great Hall because there weren't as many people there, but she could still hear it each time she stopped to move someone she had overlooked, or to glance behind her, which she did with increasing frequency. She had the strongest feeling that someone was watching her, yet as far as she knew, she was the only one awake in the entire castle.

"Is anyone there?" she called out once, but the only response was silence.

Queen Karolina's eyes were moving behind their lids when Annie knelt beside her. "Mother," she said, hesitating only a moment before placing her hand on the queen's shoulder.

"Mmm," the queen murmured, frowning slightly.

"Mother," she said again, giving the queen's shoulder a shake. "I have to talk to you."

"Whatizzit?" her mother mumbled, opening one eye a crack.

"It's the curse. Gwendolyn pricked her finger on a spinning wheel and now everyone's asleep. There must be something I can do."

"There is," said her mother. "Lemme go back to sleep."

"In a minute. I need you to help me remember exactly what the curse said. First that wicked fairy said that if Gwennie pricked her finger on a spinning wheel, she'd die. That's right, isn't it, Mother?"

Annie gave her mother another shake when she didn't answer. The queen, whose hair had begun to turn gray, muttered, "That's right. The fairy Voracia."

"And then that fairy with the revolting name stood up and changed the curse."

"Sweetness N Light. Lives in the Garden of Happiness."

"That's right! She changed the curse so that instead of dying, Gwennie would sleep for a hundred years."

"And wake when the love of her life kisses her on the lips," said the queen. "She said he has to be a prince. Won't work otherwise."

"I can't do much about the hundred years, but I can find a prince," Annie said. "Maybe he'll be able to help me with the hundred years thing."

"Go get Digby. He can kiss her," her mother replied.

Annie frowned. "I will if I have to, but that man is such a twit."

"Maybe so," the queen murmured as her daughter took her hand away. And once again the only sound was breathing.

Annie got to her feet and looked around the room. The ladies would have to stay where they were; she wasn't about to take them all back to their beds the way she had Gwendolyn. Even her mother's room was too far to take her.

She was about to leave the room when she noticed the piece of parchment that her sister had dropped. Gwendolyn couldn't read, so it was no surprise that she hadn't even glanced at the parchment. Annie, however, had made a point of learning to read and write. In fact, she had tried to learn many things that Gwendolyn couldn't do, mostly because she had no desire to compete with her sister in all the things she could do perfectly. Where Gwendolyn was as light on her feet as thistledown, and was the belle of every ball, Annie had crept away to learn dancing from the Gypsies, who didn't care how gracefully she could twirl on her toes. Gwendolyn rode sidesaddle like a lady and wore beautiful clothes. Annie put on boys' clothes and had the stable master teach her how to ride bareback. She had a groom teach her how to juggle, something Gwendolyn would never have considered doing. An old soldier taught Annie how to handle a bow and arrow. She made friends with the servants' children and asked them to teach her how to swim in the

Crystal River and catch fish from its bank. Every time she discovered something that Gwendolyn couldn't do, Annie tried to learn how to do it.

There were many things that Gwendolyn could do perfectly. There were many more that Annie could do very, very well. Unfortunately, reading the writing on the piece of paper wasn't one of them. It took her a minute of scrutinizing the florid writing with all its curlicues and whorls before she was able to make out the simple message. *Happy Birthday* was all it said, but the writing was so fancy that it looked as if there might be more.

Annie had been so worried about everyone in the castle that it hadn't occurred to her to wonder who had sent the spinning wheel. She'd assumed that the evil fairy must have sent it, but few fairies were able to write, and she'd never heard of any sending notes. The note was on nice enough parchment, but it was the kind her mother might have had, certainly nothing fairy-made.

She turned the note over, hoping there might have been some indication of who had sent it. When there wasn't anything else on the parchment, she bent down beside the trunk and examined it down to the smallest detail. It didn't look like fairy work. Although it was beautifully made, she saw a few places on the bottom where the marks of the adze hadn't been smoothed away; a trunk made by a fey craftsman would have been flawless. The man who had delivered it had appeared human as well and not like someone an evil fairy might have sent. Whoever had sent the trunk had been human, not fairy, and that was the most puzzling part. As far as Annie knew, neither Treecrest nor Gwendolyn had any human enemies.

CHAPTER 3

ANNIE STAYED IN THE CASTLE for the rest of the day. She made sure that everyone was safe and comfortable, from the highest nobles down to the boy who cleaned the pots for the scullery maids. She put out all the fires in the fireplaces, lifted the bucket from the well that was dangling from a sleeping groom's hands, and tried, unsuccessfully, to close the drawbridge facing the town. The climbing roses kept the drawbridge from moving, so Annie walked along the battlements to see how far the roses had encroached on the castle grounds. She was relieved to see that they had stopped on the other side of the moat and hadn't come any closer than the portcullis on either of the two drawbridges.

Annie was standing on the battlement facing the road into town when she noticed movement in the distance. The roses had overgrown the road for nearly a quarter mile, but beyond that it looked as if people were gathering. Wagons heading to the castle had stopped on the road, unable to get past roses that had grown higher than the horses' heads. Men on horseback were milling around the wagons, gesturing to one another and pointing at the castle.

Annie was concerned about what could happen to the sleeping inhabitants of the castle, but until now it hadn't occurred to her that the rest of her parents' subjects might be in danger as well. With the king asleep and not likely to wake any time soon, Treecrest had no one to make important decisions. And because most of his army was garrisoned in the castle, they were sound asleep as well, leaving only the soldiers currently on patrol to protect the people from bands of thieves, marauding trolls, and flocks of harpies. Annie wished she could get in touch with even one patrol, but she had no idea how to find any of them. If only there was someone she could turn to for help! She was sure that her uncle Rupert would come if she could get a message to him, but he was commanding the forces stationed at Delaroo Pass, high in the White Mountains. Even if he could leave someone else in charge of keeping the mountain trolls from entering the pass, it would take at least a month for word to reach him, then another month for him to make his way through the dragon territory that lay at the base of the mountains and cross the land that was said to be the most dangerous in all the kingdom. Annie didn't think she had that much time. Once word got out that the curse had taken its toll, unscrupulous people and nasty creatures would be pouring into the kingdom.

Annie's eyes grew wide as another horrible thought came to mind. Without the king's army, other kingdoms could invade Treecrest and be in control of the kingdom long before her family woke. Her parents could open their eyes to find themselves prisoners in their own kingdom. If Annie were to locate a prince to kiss her sister and wake everyone in the castle, she would have to do it quickly or the kingdom would be lost. Too bad she'd never traveled more than a few minutes' ride from the castle and knew only what rumor and books had told her about the rest of the kingdom.

Annie's first inclination was to start on her journey right away, but it was almost dusk and she wasn't ready to go. Deciding that she'd leave as early as she could in the morning, she went to the kitchen and collected food to take with her, then ate some cold ham and cheese and drank a cup of cider before returning to her room for the night. Although she had seen for herself that she was the only person awake in the castle, she felt uneasy and dragged a heavy trunk in front of her door to block it.

She was up before dawn the next morning after a restless night spent starting at every creak of the castle walls and whisper of a breeze outside her window. The sound of the wind chimes was so faint in her room that she could barely hear it, but the moment she opened the door it grew louder, serving as another reminder of everything that had happened the day before.

Dressed in the boy's tunic and breeches that she had worn when she learned how to ride, she tucked her hair inside a boy's cap, packed a gown, a few coins, and the other items she planned to take with her into a worn leather satchel and returned to the chamber where her mother still slept. Annie checked on her mother and sister. Reassured that they were sleeping peacefully, she went down the stairs to see her father, who, like everyone else in the castle, hadn't moved since the day before.

It felt odd creeping around in her father's private meeting room while he and his nobles were there, but she needed one of the maps kept rolled up on a row of narrow shelves. Finding the map of Treecrest and the surrounding kingdoms, Annie kissed her father on the cheek, something he never would have allowed when he was awake. He woke only briefly at her touch, but not enough to know that she was there.

The king was already snoring again when she pulled the tapestry away from the wall and reached for the latch of the hidden door. The fabric was heavy against her back as she slipped behind it and entered the secret passage that only members of the royal family knew existed. Wrinkling her nose at the musty smell, she stepped onto the landing and pulled the door closed behind her. It was dark inside the passage, but she'd been this way before. With the flint she'd brought with her clutched tightly in her hand, Annie patted the rough wall beside her until she found one of the torches kept for emergencies. She used the flint to light the torch, and descended the circular stairway that led down past the lower floors and through the center of the dungeon. Closed off from everything around it, the stairwell had little ventilation and the air felt damp and heavy.

After what seemed like forever, she reached the last step and the long, low tunnel that led out of the castle. Years before, a magic spell had been placed on the tunnel to keep it intact; Annie didn't dare linger for fear that her lack of magic might make the tunnel unsound. She walked holding the torch in front of her, relieved that she could no longer hear either the tinkling of the chimes or the collective breathing of the sleepers in the castle.

When the floor began to angle up, she hurried, anxious to get out of the tunnel. She finally emerged into a small cave and pushed aside the undergrowth that hid it from view of anyone passing by in the forest. Stepping out of the cave, she raised her face to the early-morning light filtering through the leaves overhead and paused to listen to the songs of birds, an ordinary sound that she'd missed while in the sleeping castle.

It occurred to her that she should go back and tell the townspeople what had happened to the king. Perhaps someone there could help her find the closest patrol or even go fetch Digby. She shouldered her satchel and tried to get her bearings. Knowing that the tunnel led straight from the castle, Annie figured out from the direction of the cave which way she'd have to go to reach the road.

She was picking her way through the bracken and fallen twigs when she heard voices up ahead and smelled bacon cooking. Although she was about to call out to them, she pressed her lips closed when she heard the tone of their voices. She drew closer, slipping as quietly as she could from tree to tree so they wouldn't see her, until she was within a stone's throw of a makeshift camp-site. A wagon was parked between her and the men, and she recognized it from the shape of the seat and the faded paint on the side as the one that had been used to deliver the trunk.

There were three men at the campsite, two of them sitting beside a smoking fire while a third held a pan of sizzling bacon over the flames. Roughly dressed and unshaven, they looked and sounded like the vagabonds she had feared would take advantage of her kingdom's helplessness.

"No one's seen that princess on the battlements yet today. What do you suppose she's doing in there?" said one of the men.

"Doesn't matter as long as she doesn't get out," replied the cook.

"How could she?" said the third man. "No one can get past those stinkin' roses. Soon as you hack 'em out, they grow back again. Can't go a foot without those things wrapping around you and tearing at your fleshy parts."

42

"Fenley's never going to stop complaining about those thorns."

"Shaddup, Twitch! You'll be the first to have a go at them the next time she makes us try. Then we'll see who's laughing when we pull the thorns out of your pudgy self."

"The old bat won't make us try to go in there again. My bet is once she sees that the princess is trapped like everybody else, she'll forget about this castle and build a new one somewhere else. That's what I would do."

"Is that bacon almost ready? I likes it limp, not that burnt stuff you always make."

Annie crept away, careful not to make a sound while the men argued behind her. There wasn't a minute to waste. She had to get Digby to come kiss Gwendolyn as soon as she could. The sooner her father woke up, the sooner he could chase away the interlopers before they could do any real damage. It sounded as if a woman had sent them, although she couldn't imagine who. Voracia wouldn't need men like that to do her work for her. But if it wasn't the wicked fairy, then who could it be?

Annie decided not to go to the town after all. If the woman didn't know that Annie had left the castle, she might think she had a lot more time to do whatever it was she had planned and not be in a hurry to do it. Realizing that by not talking to the townspeople, Annie might be buying her father a little more time, she turned away from the road to the village and headed east to Shimshee, the kingdom where Digby's family ruled.

Because much of Annie's childhood had been spent exploring the land around the castle, she knew this part of the forest, including the location of a little-traveled path that would take her in the general direction that she wanted to go. She walked for most of the morning and didn't stop even when her stomach started to growl. Taking out the bread and cheese she had packed in the satchel, she continued to walk even as she tore off a hunk of each. Intent on putting the rest away, she didn't notice the old woman standing in her path until she'd almost run into her.

"You wouldn't have any food to spare for a starving old woman, would you, dearie?" the old woman asked. "It's been three days since I had my last bite to eat and I—"

"Sure," said Annie, who was more concerned with getting to Shimshee than she was in talking to strangers. "Here," she said, handing her the food she'd already torn off. "I'm sorry I can't stay to talk, but I'm in a hurry and—"

"I ask for food and you give me this?" the old woman said, sniffing the cheese and looking at it with disdain. "I wouldn't give this to my dog, if I had one."

Annie watched aghast as the old woman pitched the bread and cheese into the underbrush. "That was perfectly good food!" Annie exclaimed. "I was about to eat that myself."

"Liar!" said the old woman. "You probably have the good stuff hidden in your satchel. And for refusing to be kind to an old woman in need..."

"I gave you my lunch!" said Annie.

"You will have to pay!" the woman concluded as she raised her hand and pointed one gnarled finger.

"You really don't want to do that," Annie told her. The old woman was already chanting something ominous about words and snakes when Annie brushed past her. "I don't have time for this," she said as she walked away. The sound of rattling bones reached her ears just before the magic hit her and bounced back to the old woman. There was an anguished cry and Annie glanced over her shoulder. Frogs, snakes, and lizards spilled from the old woman's mouth as she tried to scream at Annie.

"You can't say that I didn't warn you," Annie said, and hurried on her way.

CHAPTER 4

AN HOUR LATER, Annie reached unfamiliar ground. She stayed on the path she thought would take her to the branch of the Crystal River that led toward Shimshee, but by late afternoon she was no longer so certain. Although the path seemed to be going in the right direction, she had yet to see or hear running water. She began to wonder if she was lost. By the time the sun began to sink behind the trees, she was sure of it.

A wolf howled somewhere in the forest and Annie remembered the story she'd heard about a wolf following a little girl and eating her grandmother. She was considering climbing a tree for the night when she smelled wood smoke. Hoping to find the home of a woodcutter, she hurried toward the source of the smoke and entered a clearing, where she found a small cottage that hummed with magic. The candles flickering in the window looked ordinary enough and the magic didn't sound like the nasty kind, so Annie tiptoed to the window and peeked inside.

An old woman with white hair and the plump, sweet face of a kindly old grandmother carried food to two small children seated at a wide plank table. She used a cane when she walked, shuffling across the floor with an unsteady gait. When Annie bumped into the shutter, breaking off a corner, the children turned in their seats and stared at her through big, dark eyes set in pale faces. They were beautiful children with silky hair the color of walnuts and dark lashes framing their eyes, but their cheeks were dirty and tear streaked, and their clothes were soiled and torn. The boy looked as if he was a few years older than the girl, but their features were similar enough that Annie thought they must be siblings.

The boy and girl appeared frightened at first, but when they saw Annie they looked at her for only a moment before shifting their attention back to the food on the table. The old woman had seen them turn their heads and had followed their gaze to Annie. She smiled now and said in a playful voice, "Nibble, nibble, little mouse. Who's that nibbling at my house?"

"I wasn't nibbling," Annie replied. "I just wanted to see if anyone was home."

"I'm here, so you're welcome to come in. Children are always welcome, especially if they're tired and hungry. I have some very yummy food cooking. It's... What did I tell you it was, little boy?"

"Rabbit stew."

"That's right. And I'm just about to take a nice berry pie out of the oven. Come in, my dear, and make yourself at home."

Annie's foot bumped something as she began to move away from the window. She bent down to see what it was and found a large chunk of striped candy. Picking it up, she realized that it was the piece of the shutter that had broken off. The air smelled like nutmeg and ginger. When she looked closer, she saw that the walls were made of gingerbread decorated with sugar dots and icing swirls.

Annie frowned as she walked toward the open door. The humming of the magic was constant and reminded her of an old lullaby. It also reminded her that the old woman was probably a witch, yet there was no indication that she was a bad witch, at least none that Annie could hear.

"Just call me Granny Bentbone, dear. So many people do."

"I'm Charlie," Annie replied, hoping that the clothing she wore made her look enough like a boy to make the name believable.

"Are you hungry, my sweet? I'm sure you must be," the woman said, ushering Annie into the cozy kitchen. "I've cooked . . . what is it again?"

"Rabbit stew," said the boy.

Annie paused for a moment to admire a peppermint

48

stick that rose from floor to ceiling. It was as big around as her waist and looked like a support post put there to hold up the roof. She glanced up and saw that other sticks acted as beams to support the candy ceiling.

"Won't you join us, dear?" The woman gestured to a stool next to the one where the little girl was perched. The stools and the table were shorter than normal, as if they had been built for children or dwarves with small bottoms. Annie smiled at the little girl as she sat down. The girl's lips parted in a shy smile, showing the gap of missing teeth. Seated on the other side of the girl, the boy nudged her and placed another piece of bread on her trencher, drawing her attention away from Annie.

Something scrabbled at the floor on the far side of the room and Annie raised her head to look around. A ladder led up to a loft across from where she was sitting. A wide cupboard painted a cheery yellow with a green vine and red and blue flowers stood beside a fireplace where a crackling fire burned. A metal door on the other side of the fireplace covered the opening for an oven big enough to fit a small ox. On the floor near the oven door there was a woven basket. Inside the basket a gray-furred animal lay staring up at Annie with beady eyes that didn't blink. It had a sharp little twitchy nose and whiskers that quivered with every breath.

"That's the biggest rat I've ever seen," Annie said under her breath.

Granny Bentbone saw where Annie was looking.

"That's my little dog...What's his name again? Just a minute, dear." The old woman walked along the wall, eyeing it closely, until she stopped suddenly and said, "I think it's...Yes, that's it. He's Fluffy. I need to feed him."

"He bites!" whispered the little girl, looking solemn.

"I bet!" Annie said, and the little girl giggled.

While Granny Bentbone cut a chunk from a wheel of cheese and set it in a dish for Fluffy, Annie peered at the wall, puzzled by the way the woman had been studying it. And then she saw them—little candy hearts, some made of pink sugar, some of yellow. They were everywhere and they all seemed to have something written on them. Annie leaned toward the one closest to her. It read:

Brush your teeth before you go to bed.

"Interesting," Annie murmured.

The little boy had been watching Annie. "She forgets things a lot," he whispered. "She reads those hearts and they tell her what to do. Sometimes she remembers things, but then she forgets them again. Can you read? We can't, although I wish I could. I'd like to know what some of those hearts say."

"So would I," Annie whispered back. The writing on the hearts was so small that she could read only those closest to her. The wall on the opposite side of the room sported dozens, some of which were covered with the tiny writing.

Granny Bentbone was carrying a mug to the cupboard when she said, "You must be lost. So many are. That's why they come this far into the forest."

Annie turned to the children seated beside her. "Were you lost?"

The little boy nodded. "I'm Tomas and this is my sister, Clara. We're here because of our new stepmother. She said we eat too much and didn't leave enough for her children, Poopsie and Wiggles."

"Why would anyone name their children Poopsie and Wiggles?" asked Annie.

"They are dogs," said Tomas. "She just calls them her children. She gave them our food to eat and put our clothes on them and called them by our names, then took us for walkies in the woods and left us there."

"We waited for Papa to come get us, but he never did," said the little girl. "So we started walking until we saw this cottage."

Fluffy brushed past Annie's legs. She grimaced and pulled her legs back, then watched him waddle to the peppermint stick post, which he began to gnaw.

"Papa probably hasn't noticed we're gone yet," Tomas told Annie. "He leaves every morning before the sun comes up and gets home after we would be in bed."

"Do you need someone to help you find your way back?" Annie asked. She was in a hurry to get to Shimshee, but if their cottage wasn't too far out of her way . . .

"We don't want to go back," said the girl. She yawned and rubbed her eyes with her fists.

"Papa wasn't our real father," said Tomas. "Our real father lived in a castle. Papa stole us away when Clara was just a baby. That's where we're going now—to find our real father."

"Don't lie, Tomas," Clara told him. "Papa will take a strap to you again if he finds out you've been telling fibs."

The little boy looked as if he wanted to say something, but instead he glanced from his sister to Annie and Granny Bentbone before turning his face away.

"I've invited them to stay here with me," said Granny Bentbone.

Annie watched the old woman pick up a big bowl of rabbit stew. She was carrying it to the table when she staggered and nearly fell. "Fluffy!" she said, wagging her finger at the rat. "You have to stay out of my way. I'm too old for such shenanigans."

"Maybe he needs to go out," said Annie. "Our dogs at home like a little exercise before they go to bed."

"What a good idea!" said Granny Bentbone. "Come along, Fluffy. A little fresh air will do us both good."

Annie waited until the old woman had shooed her "dog" outside, then she sprang to her feet and ran to the wall. She was curious about the candy hearts; reading them might be a good way to learn about Granny Bentbone. The first few weren't much help.

Remember to feed Fluffy!
If you are hungry—eat!
You sit on the white pot.
You cook with the black pot.

If children come to the cottage, invite them in.
Do not let adults in!

"That's odd," Annie said to herself. "Is she afraid of something?" The next heart was a reminder that the dog was named Fluffy. The note after that made Annie feel as if a cold finger were tracing her spine.

When children come to the cottage,
lock them in the cages at night.

"And this woman does what these things say? That's horrible!" It took Annie only a moment to peel the candy heart off the wall and stuff it into her pocket. Hearing Granny Bentbone at the door talking to Fluffy, she knew that she didn't have long to read, and there were still dozens of candy hearts on the wall.

A heart on a door leading off from the kitchen simply read *Cages*. The next heart was bigger than the rest, as if it was more important.

Look in the room marked "cages."
If there is a child in there—feed it.

You want it to be fat.
If it is fat, cook it.

Annie shuddered and glanced at the children sitting at the table. The food piled on the plates in front of them suddenly had a new and horrible significance. She broke her fingernail peeling the big heart off the wall and crushed it into dust once it was in her pocket. The door was already opening when she peeled off one last candy heart.

Find recipes for children in the big
blue book in the cupboard.

Annie shoved the candy heart into her pocket even as she hurried back to her seat. She broke it with her thumbnail and crumbled it while Granny Bentbone came back into the house alone.

Clara stopped licking the icing off a piece of cake long enough to ask, "Where's Fluffy?"

"Who?" asked Granny Bentbone. She stared at the children, puzzled. "What are you doing here? Do I know you?"

"It's us, Granny Bentbone," said Annie as she got to her feet. "Charlie and Tomas and Clara. You said we should go to bed in the loft upstairs, remember? We were just waiting to say good night."

"Oh, yes. I remember now. Good night, children."

"But …," said Clara.

"Good night, Granny," said Annie as she pulled the children from their seats. When Clara tried to protest, Annie shushed her, saying, "If you go to bed now, I'll tell you a story."

Tomas saw the look on Annie's face. "Let's go, Clara," he said, and helped Annie get his little sister up the ladder.

Annie had brought a candle from the table, and after closing the trapdoor, she used the candle's light to find her way around the loft. There were no beds, nor had she really expected to find any, but there were baskets of well-worn clothes and a few old toys.

"Where are we going to sleep?" asked Clara, scrubbing at her sleepy eyes with her knuckles. "I want to go see Granny Bentbone."

"You'll see her in the morning," said Annie. "Granny Bentbone is going to bed now, too."

While the children watched, Annie moved the baskets out of the way. Taking clothes from the baskets, she spread them on the floor so that the children could lie down. "There you go," she said, helping Clara onto the makeshift bed. "That's much better than sleeping on the ground outside. Here, I found this." She handed the little girl a doll.

The doll's clothes were soiled and it was missing one arm, but Clara looked as if she'd been given a treasure. Her entire face lit up and she took the doll, clutching it to her chest. Her eyelids were drifting shut when Annie covered her with an old cloak, and she was asleep before Annie kissed her on the cheek.

"So much for a bedtime story," Annie murmured. "Tomas," she said, looking up. "I need to talk to you."

Tomas followed her to the other side of the loft, picking his way just as quietly around the baskets. "I read some of those hearts," Annie whispered. "Granny Bentbone is not a good person. She means to hurt us if we stay here. We have to leave at first light."

"Why don't we leave now?" asked Tomas.

"Where would we go? It isn't safe in the woods at night. We'll be fine here until morning. Granny Bentbone can't climb a ladder with that cane. Besides, there's something I have to do after she goes to sleep."

"I'll go with you."

Annie shook her head. "I need you to stay here and take care of Clara. She'd be frightened if she woke up and found that she was alone. You should lie down and rest. I'll be back before you know it."

"What if you aren't?" Tomas asked, his voice wavering.

"Then you take Clara out of here as soon as you hear the birds singing outside and run as far from this cottage as you can. But don't worry. I promise I'll be back."

Tomas didn't look as if he believed her, so after tucking him in beside Clara, Annie assured him again, then didn't leave until he had fallen asleep as well.

When it had been quiet downstairs for some time, Annie crept to the trapdoor and lifted it ever so slowly. The only light came from the fire in the fireplace and a candle that Granny Bentbone had forgotten to blow out. No one was there, so Annie climbed down the ladder, pausing at each rung to listen for even the smallest sound.

Picking up the candle, she tiptoed to the door marked "Cages" and took a deep breath. Annie opened the door a crack. When she didn't hear anything, she pushed it wider and exhaled in a sigh of relief. There were four big cages in the room and all of them were empty.

Annie closed the door just as quietly as she had opened it and turned to face the room. There were so many candy hearts and she had no idea how much time she had. Although it was hours until daylight, if the old woman was a light sleeper, she might not have much time at all.

While the candle burned lower, Annie crept around the room, reading the candy hearts. Most of them were reminders to Granny Bentbone to keep herself clean and fed, but a few mentioned recipes and the location of certain pots and pans. Annie took these down and crushed them. When she'd read all of the hearts, she crossed to the cupboard and began looking for the cookbook. She found a box of blank candy hearts first, along with a small pot of icing and a quill pen. Taking them out of the cupboard, she carried them to the table and sat down. It didn't take her long to write her own messages on the candy hearts.

Do not eat meat. It makes you bloated.
Eat vegetables, pastries, and candy.
They will make you happy.

If children come to your door, give them
food and send them on their way.

A rat is not a dog. Do not feed the rats!

When she finished, Annie used the icing to stick the hearts to the walls where she'd already taken others down. After putting away the rest of the hearts as well as the pot of icing and the pen, she continued rifling through the cupboard and found the cookbook behind a cracked clay pitcher.

Annie didn't want to touch the book, but she knew what she had to do. Crinkling her mouth with distaste, she picked up the cookbook and carried it to the fireplace, where she laid it on top of the dying fire. The flames flared up and one of the logs beneath it broke with a loud *crack!* Annie was climbing back up the ladder when Granny Bentbone came into the room.

"Who are you?" the old woman demanded. "What are you doing in my house? Are you a thief? Did you come to rob me?"

"No, Granny Bentbone. I'm your guest, remember? I just came downstairs for a drink of water."

"Oh," the old woman said. "I don't remember where the water is."

"That's all right. I can wait until morning."

Annie could feel the old woman's eyes boring into her back as she climbed the ladder. Her hands were shaking when she closed the trapdoor and she didn't move until she heard the floor below creak as Granny Bentbone returned to her room. Her heart was still pounding when she lay down beside Clara, but the sound of the little girl's soft breathing helped calm her and she dozed, only to startle awake at every noise. Suddenly the floor beneath her groaned like an old man with an aching back. Annie's eyes shot open. Although the floor had been level when she lay down, it was now sagging under her weight. She was confused until she remembered that magic was holding the gingerbread together. Her presence was diminishing the room's magic, making the whole thing unstable.

The floor creaked when Annie stood up. Afraid to move for a moment, she waited to make sure that it was sound enough to hold them before waking the children. She woke Tomas first, shaking him by the shoulder until his eyes blinked open. "We have to go," she whispered. "Make sure that Clara knows she has to be quiet."

Tomas nodded and woke his little sister with a nudge. They whispered together while Annie moved toward the trapdoor and raised it just enough to see down. When she was sure that Granny Bentbone wasn't there, she led the way down the stairs and to the door.

Annie had her hand on the latch when Clara said in a loud voice, "I don't want to go yet. I'm hungry. Can't we have breakfast first?"

"Shh! Clara, I told you to be quiet!" Tomas told her.

"I wasn't being loud," said Clara. "I just—"

"What are you children doing here?" Granny Bentbone said from the door to her room. "How did you get out of your cages?"

Annie shoved the door open and pushed the children across the threshold as the old woman hobbled toward them. "Remember what I told you, Tomas," Annie told him. "Run!"

"No!" shrieked Granny Bentbone as the children raced across the clearing that surrounded the house and into the forest beyond.

The old woman moved faster than Annie had thought possible. While Annie was reaching for the satchel that she'd left beside the door, Granny Bentbone hustled across the room and whacked her with the cane. Annie stumbled back until she bumped into the peppermint support post.

"Don't think I don't know what you're doing," the old woman said, shaking her cane at Annie. "You came here to let those children out of my cages. Well, that's fine and dandy, because now I have you to take their place!"

60

Annie recalled what Tomas had said about the woman remembering some things sometimes. If only it hadn't happened now! She was wondering how she'd get past the old woman and her stick when she realized that she could feel the hard candy post softening under her hand. Leaning back, she wrapped her fingers as far as they would go around the post and squeezed. The candy softened faster now, the surface dissolving just like it did in a child's mouth.

Granny Bentbone stepped closer, ranting as she tried to force Annie toward the room with the cages. Annie squeezed the peppermint post, digging her fingers into its sticky surface. Suddenly the post cracked and buckled, sending a chunk of the ceiling crashing down in a shower of sugar dust. Annie jumped aside, nearly knocking over the surprised old woman, who staggered and fell across a bench.

While Granny Bentbone screeched and wailed, Annie darted to the door, grabbed her satchel, and ran out into the night.

CHAPTER 5

ANNIE DIDN'T STOP RUNNING until she reached the edge of the forest and began to creep from one tree to the next, hoping to find the children there waiting for her. No voice responded to Annie's calls, no figure emerged from the darkness under the trees. Although Annie was afraid of what she might encounter in the woods at night, she was too worried about the children being alone in the dark to give up. If the full moon hadn't been out, she wouldn't have been able to continue searching, but there was enough light that she was able to make a complete circuit of the woods fronting the clearing, stumbling over roots while twigs scratched her face and snagged her clothes and hair.

Annie heard the fairies before she saw them. Exhausted, she had stopped to lean against a tree for a moment's rest when she heard sprightly music and the sound of laughter. Thinking she might finally have found the children, she followed the music deeper into the woods. Rounding an old oak, Annie nearly stumbled on the fairy ring. Made of red mushrooms sprinkled with white polka dots, the ring was aglow with the light of fireflies. At one end of the circle, a strange little group of musicians created the music. Crickets chirped, frogs croaked, and birds sang while squirrels thumped out the beat with their hind paws. Fairies no taller than Annie's little finger were dancing in the circle, hopping and skipping in time to the music.

Annie backed away, hoping she hadn't been seen. After hearing so many stories about the mischief that fairies could do, she had no desire to meet them. It was too late, however, for a cry went up before she'd taken a second step, and suddenly the air around her was filled with curious fairies, their brightly colored wings fanning the air.

"It's a boy!" cried a fairy dressed all in yellow.

"No, it's not," said the fairy beside her. "It's a girl dressed as a boy. Can't you tell the difference?"

The first fairy shook her head. "They all look alike to me."

"She's come to join our dance!" cried a third fairy.

"Step into the ring!" sang out a chorus of fairy voices. "You can dance with us until dawn!"

"No, I can't," Annie hurried to say. "Thank you for asking me, but I'm too tired to dance with anyone. I just want to—" She staggered into the ring when a dozen fairies pushed her from behind.

"Dance like this!" a fairy dressed all in green cried, twirling on her toes.

"No, like this!" another wearing a hat of moss shouted as he flailed his arms and hopped.

A fairy with pink hair and a dress made of pansy petals flew into the air in front of her to say, "It doesn't matter how you do it, just dance!"

Annie sighed. She was so tired that all she wanted to do was lie down and go to sleep, but she doubted the fairies would let her. Perhaps if she danced with them for a few minutes... Shuffling around the ring, she followed the fairy in front of her. She flapped her hands now and then to make it look more like dancing than walking, but paid little attention to the dancing fairies other than to try not to step on them. The fairies seemed to think that was enough and continued to cavort around her. After a time her eyelids drooped and her pace slowed until she was doing little more than swaying on her feet.

She scarcely felt the fairy who landed on her shoulder until he shouted, "Wake up!" directly into her ear.

Annie's eyes shot open as she clapped her hand to her head, missing the fairy by inches when he flew out of the way.

"You have to dance!" the pink fairy shouted, stamping her foot on the toe of Annie's shoe. "No one's allowed to sleep in our fairy ring!"

"I'm sorry," Annie said, stifling a yawn. "I told you I

was tired. I'll just lie down over there and get out of your way so you can dance."

The fairy wearing the mossy cap fluttered his wings and darted up to hover in front of Annie. "We never said you could sleep. You sleep in the daytime, not now. If you're too tired to dance with us, we can help you." Opening a tiny pouch, the fairy flew above Annie and sprinkled sparkly dust over her head and shoulders.

Annie sneezed and rubbed her nose with the back of her hand. "That isn't going to do anything."

"Why isn't she dancing?" asked a fairy with white hair like a dandelion puff when Annie didn't move.

The fairy with the mossy cap flew down to look in Annie's eyes. "I don't know. I used the right fairy dust, but her eyes aren't glazing over."

"She has to dance! Everyone has to dance when we tell them to!" said another fairy.

"Honestly, your dust won't work on me," Annie began, but the fairies didn't seem to be listening. When she tried to step out of the ring, a group of them gathered in front of her and batted their wings in her face while others sprinkled her with more dust. The fairy dust settled on her shoulders like drifts of pink and purple dandruff. It trickled into her collar and made her itch. She opened her mouth to tell them how useless it was to sprinkle fairy dust on her, but when she inhaled she started coughing so hard that she couldn't stop. Dust fell off her with each cough, making the ground around her sparkle.

"She's wasting our dust!" cried a fairy with blue hair. Scowling, the fairy flew close enough to tweak Annie's nose. Annie swatted at him, knocking the fairy away.

"I'll teach her!" shouted the dandelion-puff fairy. Flying at head height, the fairy pointed her finger and ordered Annie to turn into a pig. The air sizzled between Annie and the fairy for just an instant before the magic rebounded and struck the fairy full force. The other fairies gasped with horror when their friend's wings disappeared and she fell to the ground grunting, a tiny pig no bigger than Annie's little finger.

Suddenly the cloud of fairies settled on Annie, pulling her hair, pinching her cheeks, and jabbing her with pine needles that they'd picked up from the forest floor.

"Get away from me!" Annie shouted. Waving her hands, she batted at the fairies, sending them tumbling through the air each time her hand made contact. She twisted and turned beneath their attack, slapping at her back and legs as she tried to rid herself of the more determined fairies, but the more she slapped, the angrier they became, until it felt as if she were caught in the midst of a swarm of bees. As the fairies became nastier, Annie squeezed her eyes shut and covered them with one of her hands, leaving only one hand free for slapping. When she

66

bumped into the old oak tree, she thought she heard a faint crunch, but didn't dare open her eyes to look.

The fairies had jabbed Annie with so many pine needles and pinched her so many times that she was sure she must be covered with tiny holes and bruises. It didn't look as if they'd ever give up, so finally in desperation she threw herself flat on the ground and began to roll. Although some of the more stubborn fairies held on, most of them let go rather than risk being squashed. She was still rolling across the uneven floor when a roar shook the forest. The fairies fled, leaving Annie alone. She lay motionless, her eyes closed as something big lumbered near enough to snuffle her face, swiping it with something warm and wet.

Now what? Annie thought. When nothing more happened, she opened one eye a crack and peered up. A huge black head blocked the moonlight. At first Annie couldn't tell what it was, just that it wasn't a fairy. It had a heavy, musky smell that was worse than wet dog, so she knew it was an animal of some sort.

When Annie didn't move, the creature grunted and poked her with its paw. Annie peeked at it again. Suddenly she knew not only what it was, but why the fairies had fled. It was a bear, and it was standing so close that its breath warmed her cheek. She would have jumped up and run away if the bear hadn't set its huge paw on her arm, pinning her down. Certain that the bear was about to eat her,

Annie was stunned when it said in a voice deeper than her father's, "Are you all right?"

"You...you can talk?" she asked, opening both eyes wide.

"Why shouldn't I?" said the bear. "I'm not really a bear. I'm Prince Beldegard, heir to the throne of Montrose."

"I can see that," Annie said. What had first been a great, shaggy head was slowly changing shape into something more refined and less fearsome. As she watched, the beast began to look less like an animal and more like a young man.

"What do you mean?" Beldegard sat back and lifted his paw to his face. His mouth dropped open when he saw that it was beginning to look like a hand. Annie thought he looked so silly that she couldn't keep from laughing. "I don't understand," said the prince. "Are you a wizard? Have you used your magic on me? This is wonderful!" Beldegard reared up so that he towered over her. "I can return home to Montrose and—"

Annie shook her head. "I'm not a wizard and I don't have any magic. It's just the opposite, in fact," she said. "Whatever spell was cast on you will fade for as long as you and I are touching. You moved away, so you're already beginning to look more like a bear again."

Beldegard, who was getting shaggier by the second, plopped down on all four feet and sidled closer to Annie. "Then I guess you're going to have to stay with me until I get rid of that dwarf." When Annie looked puzzled, he sat down beside her and set his paw on her hand. "A nasty dwarf wants my treasure. He turned me into a bear to get me out of the way. I suppose he thought I wouldn't remember anything if I was a bear, but he was wrong. I've spent the last two years protecting my treasure from spring to fall. In the winter when the ground is frozen and I know that my treasure is safe, I sleep on the hearth of a kindly old widow and her two young daughters. I'm going to marry one of the daughters once the dwarf is dead and I'm a prince again. She doesn't know it yet, so don't mention it when you see her. You seemed comfortable enough lying on the ground; sleeping in the woods shouldn't be a problem for you. It won't be for long—I've been hunting the dwarf and I'm getting closer to catching him every day. I haven't decided if I'm going to eat him or throw him off a cliff, but once I take care of the dwarf, I'll be a prince again and will reward you handsomely."

"I'm sorry," said Annie, "but I can't possibly stay with you. It's urgent that I get to Shimshee as soon as I can. I need to find Prince Digby and bring him back to my kingdom. I'm a princess, and my task is as important to me as yours is to you."

The bear, who'd begun to look like a man again, shook his slightly less shaggy head. "You're a princess? I thought you were a boy."

Annie took off her cap, letting her long hair fall around her face.

"Even so," said the bear prince, "you don't look like a princess to me. You look so...ordinary."

Annie sighed. "I know. Magic doesn't work on me, remember? That includes all the spells that would have made me beautiful. I'm from Treecrest, and my sister, Gwendolyn—"

"I've heard of Princess Gwendolyn. She's said to be even more beautiful than most princesses."

"That's her all right. She's one of the people I'm trying to help. I'm sorry I can't make you turn back permanently, but I was wondering if you could do something for me. I helped two children escape from an old woman who I think was a witch. The children are wandering in these woods now, and I haven't been able to find them. If you come across a boy named Tomas and his little sister, Clara, could you take them to the cottage of that kindly old widow and keep them safe?"

Beldegard's nostrils flared. "Children shouldn't be alone in these woods! But don't you worry. I'll see if I can find them and when I do I'll take them to the widow's cottage. I love children. I can't wait to have five or six myself." Taking Annie's hand with his not-quite paw, the prince pressed a kiss on her palm and said, "Even if you can't stay with me, I'm glad I was able to feel partly human again, if only for a little while. I've been a bear for so long that I was beginning to worry that I might lose touch with my human side."

"Your Majesty, I want you to slowly and carefully

back away from the monster," said a voice from behind Annie.

Annie peered toward the direction of the voice but couldn't see a thing.

"You don't look like a monster," Prince Beldegard whispered to her, "so whoever that is must be talking about me."

"Who is that?" Annie called into the dark. "I'm not in any danger; you needn't do whatever it is you have planned. This is a prince who's been turned into a bear."

"Right, and I'm a tree who's been turned into a man."

"Really?" asked Annie. "I'd like to see that."

"No, not really!"

"This is funny," said the bear prince, "because she's a girl who looks like a boy."

"Your eyesight must have been affected. She doesn't look anything like a boy. What's your name, Prince?" the voice asked.

"I'm Beldegard, heir to the throne of Montrose," called the prince, who was looking more and more like a man every minute. By now his ears had moved down to the side of his head and his teeth were only slightly too big for his mouth.

"A greedy dwarf cast a spell on him," Annie called, then turned to Beldegard and whispered, "That isn't the dwarf's voice, is it?"

The prince shook his head just like a bear might have done. "The dwarf sounds a lot whinier than that."

"Are you all right, Princess?" said the voice. A figure stepped out of the darkness into a patch of moonlight. Annie could see it was a young man with his cap pulled low over his forehead. Even though he was talking to Annie, he kept his sword pointed unwaveringly at Prince Beldegard.

"Do you know this man?" asked the bear prince.

"I don't think so," said Annie, "although his voice is kind of familiar."

"Don't worry. I'll keep you safe. A prince-turned-bear can still have enough honor to protect a fair young maiden, even if you aren't as beautiful as your sister."

"Thanks, I think," Annie said, pulling her hand away.

"That was rude," the young man said. "You should never tell a young lady that she isn't as pretty as her sister. Now, about that dwarf...He wouldn't happen to have a long white beard and a mustache that looks like it's growing out of his nose, would he? I saw one by the creek back there carrying a leather bag that jingled when he dropped it."

"That's him!" roared Prince Beldegard, pushing himself to his feet. "Just let me get my paws on that knobby-headed little..."

Annie didn't hear the rest of what he planned to do, as his words were lost when he crashed through the underbrush. "So much for keeping me safe," she muttered, listening to the bear prince's passage through the forest. Glancing up at the young man, she decided that she was too stiff and sore to stand. "This has been a very long day and I'm too tired to even think about running. Are you going to whack me with your sword or are you going to put it down?"

"Huh?" said the young man. "Oh, this!" He moved the sword to the side so that it was no longer aiming in Annie's general direction, then yanked his cap from his head and bowed. "It's me, Your Majesty. It's Liam. You do remember me, don't you?"

CHAPTER 6

Forgetting all the lessons in decorum she had ever received, Annie shrieked, jumped to her feet, and threw herself at Liam. Surprised, the young man staggered and dropped his sword in the dirt.

"I am so happy to see you!" Annie exclaimed, wrapping her arms around him.

"Uh, yes, I'm happy to see you, too." Liam didn't seem to know what to do. He stood there, stiff and uncomfortable, looking down at the princess's face beaming up at him.

It took a moment for Annie to notice just how uncomfortable he looked. Suddenly self-conscious, she let go and took a step back, grateful that it was too dark for him to see the blush reddening her cheeks.

"How did you find me?" she asked, straightening her rumpled clothes.

"I came across your trail in the woods outside the castle."

"So you came after me?"

Liam nodded. "I have a knack for tracking. I couldn't just let my princess go wandering around in the woods all by herself."

"I'm *your* princess now?" Annie asked, a warm feeling starting in the pit of her stomach.

"You became my princess when I took an oath as a royal guard. Nothing can change that," said Liam. "What happened back there, anyway? I'd gone into town on an errand for Captain Sterling, and by the time I came back a thicket of roses had grown up around the castle. I tried to hack my way through, but it was impossible."

"It was Gwendolyn's curse. She touched a spinning wheel even after we were so careful to keep them out."

"I thought it was something like that. From what I could see, the guards weren't patrolling the parapets or standing by the gate. I don't know much about roses, but those were obviously the magical kind. Were you inside when it happened?"

"I was in the room with Gwendolyn and her ladies. Everyone is fine, but unless we can break the curse, they'll be asleep for a hundred years."

"You're still awake because of that whole thing about you and magic, aren't you? The other guards were talking about it after you found that witch with the spinning wheel. They said that magic can't touch you."

Annie sighed. "No, but it was awful seeing everyone else fall asleep. I didn't know what to do, so I woke my mother long enough to ask for her advice. I'm on my way to Shimshee to get Prince Digby. He just needs to kiss Gwennie and everyone will wake up."

"You do realize that you're nowhere near the road to Shimshee?"

"I was afraid of that. I got lost yesterday and came across a cottage where this horrible woman lived." Annie yawned, covering her mouth with her hand. She was so tired that her eyes were watering.

"You need to rest," Liam said. Shrugging out of the straps that held a sack on his back, he pulled out a thin blanket and spread it on the ground.

"There were two children," Annie murmured as Liam led her to the blanket. "And a rat. The old woman thought it was a dog. And then there were fairies…"

"In the cottage?" asked Liam.

Annie curled up on the blanket and tucked her hands beneath her cheek. "No, in the ring," she mumbled. "And then they got mad and the bear came…"

"And then what happened?" Liam asked as he settled on the ground with his back against a tree and his sword on his lap.

Annie didn't answer; she'd fallen asleep, feeling safe

for the first time since her sister had touched the spinning wheel.

჻

When Annie woke the next morning, Liam was sitting with his back against the tree with his eyes closed, a knife in his hand, and the sword balanced on his knees. She sat up and rubbed the grit from her eyes, pleased that he was really there and hadn't been a dream. Although she hadn't known Liam for long, he was someone from home and therefore familiar. His presence made Annie feel more secure and a little less worried about her trip to Shimshee.

Moving as quietly as she could so she wouldn't wake him, she tiptoed away from the blanket, looking for privacy behind some shrubs. She hadn't gone far when she thought she saw something glinting between the leaves of a river birch. Only a few steps farther and she saw a lake with the early-morning sunlight sparkling on its surface.

After making use of the shrubs, Annie went down to the lake to splash water on her face. She was still bending over the water when the reflection of a horse appeared behind her. Annie sat back on her heels, surprised that she hadn't heard the animal approach. When the beast pawed the ground, Annie jumped up and backed away. It was a handsome animal with a long, curved neck and a well-shaped head, but its eyes had a fierce look to them, and she could just make out the faint twanging sound of unfriendly magic.

The horse reached toward her with its head and bumped her on the shoulder. Annie took another step back. The sound had grown louder with the horse's touch, and Annie knew that it was trying to use its magic to make her do something. "Oh, no you don't," Annie said. Her gaze fell on a big stick and she reached for it even as the horse took another step toward her, its ears flicking with interest. Brandishing the stick in front of her, Annie walked away from the lake, careful to keep her eyes on the horse.

When it saw that she was getting away, the horse put its ears back and trotted after her. She dodged out of the way when it opened its mouth and lunged, trying to bite her. In that instant, Annie saw that its teeth weren't blunt like a horse's, but sharp and pointed like a carnivore's.

"You're not a horse!" Annie exclaimed, wielding the stick. "You're a kelpie! I'm not going anywhere with you. Get away from me, you nasty beast. You're not carrying me to your lake to drown me!"

"Annie, is that you?" Liam called from farther in the forest. "Stay right there. I'll come to you."

The kelpie's head swung around at the sound of Liam's voice. Afraid that the beast would try to go after the young guard, Annie shouted and ran at it with the stick. The kelpie reared and struck out with its forelegs so that she had to back away, then galloped past her, moving between the trees as easily as if on an open road. Annie chased after it, dodging branches and roots. By the time she got there, the kelpie was already facing Liam.

"Don't!" Annie cried as Liam reached a hand toward the kelpie.

Before she could get closer, the animal knelt beside the young man. In one smooth movement, Liam vaulted onto the kelpie's back.

"Liam, no!" Annie shouted, still running toward him.

Liam grinned and offered her his hand. "Come here, Annie, I'll help you up. I have a ride for us. We'll get to Shimshee in no time now."

"Get off, Liam!" Annie shouted as the animal wheeled around and started back toward the lake. "It's not a horse. It's a kelpie!"

Startled, Liam looked like he was trying to dismount, but before he could swing his leg over the kelpie's side, the beast began to gallop. Annie started to run after them and tripped over something on the ground. Liam's pack was lying where he'd left it, along with his sword and knife. He was defenseless, and unless she did something fast, he was going to drown.

Ignoring the lash of the twigs on her face, Annie followed the kelpie to the lake. She ran as fast as she could, but the kelpie had already entered the lake when she arrived. Galloping through the shallow water, it began swimming once the water reached its chest. Annie could see that Liam was still struggling to get off. The kelpie's

79

magic was holding him on, however, and both man and beast had begun to sink beneath the surface.

Kicking off her shoes, Annie waded to the deeper water and dove in headfirst. "Go back!" Liam shouted as he struggled to hold his head above the surface.

Annie swam faster, reaching out toward Liam with one hand, then the other in sure, steady strokes. She lost sight of him when the kelpie completely submerged, but when she ducked her head and looked around, she spotted the kelpie only yards away. She swam toward it; the kelpie saw her and struck out with its hooves, catching her with a glancing blow that spun her around in the water and left her dazed, disoriented, and out of air.

Annie surfaced long enough to get a breath before diving again. She saw the kelpie swimming toward the edge of a drop-off. Liam was trying to dismount, but the beast's magic kept him on its back as surely as if he'd been glued there. Annie could tell that he was struggling for air and was beginning to look frantic. Afraid that she would lose Liam for good if they reached the deeper water, Annie swam as fast as she could, reaching them just as the beast was about to plunge over the edge. A few more quick strokes and she grasped the kelpie's flowing tail, which she used to pull herself closer.

The kelpie spun around and snapped at Annie. Grabbing a fistful of its mane, she used the momentum of its next lunge to pull herself up and flip over its back, landing in front of Liam. When he didn't seem to notice her, Annie feared she might already have lost him.

It took only seconds for Annie's presence to affect the kelpie. At first it twisted its neck and tried to snap at her, but then it faltered and shook its head as if something was wrong. Showing the whites of its eyes, it suddenly began to act as if it, too, were running out of air. With two powerful kicks, the kelpie surfaced. It was gasping for air, its nostrils flaring, when Annie pulled Liam from its back.

Although his feeble flailing made it harder to swim while dragging him, Annie was just happy that he was alive. When his flailing became strong enough to drag them both under the water, however, she began to lose patience with him. "Stop struggling or I'll have to knock you out," Annie told him, even though she doubted that she could carry through with such a threat. For one thing, they were too far from shore and there was nothing to use . . .

"Let go," said Liam. "You don't need to rescue me. I can swim."

"I'm sure you can," said Annie, "but you're weak as a kitten now. I told you, stop flailing."

Suddenly Liam went limp and became a dead weight in her arms. Annie shook him, worried that the kelpie might have given him a serious injury that hadn't been fatal until now. "Are you all right?" she asked.

"You told me to stop moving, so I did," said Liam, grinning up at her.

Annie let him go for a fraction of a second. His face went under and when he came back up, he spluttered and spit out a mouthful of water. "If you're rescuing me, would you mind not dunking me like that?"

"Sorry. I had to change arms. You're no lightweight, you know."

"I'm fine now. You can let go."

"Okay." Annie let go and Liam sank, but he didn't go far. They had reached the shallow water and he hit the sandy bottom as soon as he kicked his feet. She smiled when he gave her a reproachful look, and glanced back toward the middle of the lake. "You can stand, can't you? That kelpie is looking this way."

Liam scrambled to his feet and staggered with his first step. Taking his hand, Annie helped him out of the water.

Satisfied that the kelpie wasn't following them, they trudged back to the campsite to collect their things. Although their clothes were dripping wet, the air was already warm and Annie wasn't cold. "Do you want to rest or change your clothes?" she asked.

Liam shook his head. "I should be asking you that. Do you have a change of clothes with you?"

"Just an old gown. I wouldn't want to try walking through a forest in it. The hem would snag on everything. It's warm enough that this should dry pretty quickly though," Annie added, squeezing the water from a sodden sleeve. She glanced up and saw that Liam was scowling down at the ground where his sword and knife still rested. "What's wrong?"

"I can't believe that kelpie fooled me like that. I've never gotten on a strange horse that just walked up to me before. And I left my knife! I could really have used that knife."

"It was part of the kelpie's magic to make you want to get on its back. The kelpie tried it on me first, but it didn't work."

"Huh," Liam grunted. "And that's supposed to make me feel better? You stood up to it and I hopped right on."

"All I was saying was that its magic couldn't affect me. I probably would have gotten on, too, if I'd been a normal person."

"Say, that's right," Liam said, his expression brightening. He bent down to gather his weapons; when he stood up he was scowling again. "You shouldn't have done it, you know. Chasing after a kelpie could have gotten you killed. You don't have magic to keep you safe."

"Neither do you," said Annie. "And if I hadn't gone after that kelpie, *you* would have been killed. You know, instead of being rude, you could just thank me for rescuing you."

"Thanks," Liam said in a begrudging kind of way. "But you still shouldn't have done it."

Annie frowned and turned her back to him as she shouldered her sack.

Closing the distance between them in three long

strides, Liam reached out and gripped her shoulder, turning her to face him. "No, I really do mean it. Thanks. Most people wouldn't have tried to help me like that." He flashed Annie a quick smile, which made him look younger and tugged at her heart in an unexpected way. She found herself wanting to see his smile again.

Annie looked into his eyes and nodded slowly. "You're welcome."

"The road is in that direction," Liam said, pointing behind her.

He led the way into the woods, stopping to hold branches so they wouldn't hit Annie and offering her his hand when they climbed steep hills or crossed streams with slippery rocks.

Annie found his thoughtfulness touching; when she was younger she'd often played in the woods with pages and stable boys who treated her like just another boy. It also made her wonder about something he'd said earlier. "Did you really mean it when you said that most people wouldn't have tried to help you? What about your family?"

"My family knows I can take care of myself, because... well, usually I can. My father always expected me to, because he made sure I knew how. Most people don't know a fraction of what he does about weapons. He taught me everything I know about them, and... See this? He gave me this sword when I was eight years old. It was too big for me then, but he was so proud when I finally learned how to use it.

"My father is old now and hasn't been able to do much ever since his horse threw him. It was a few years ago, but his leg never healed right and he has days now where he's in so much pain that he can't do much of anything."

"What about the rest of your family?"

"I've never gotten along with my mother or my brother. It wouldn't occur to either of them to help me, even if I was on fire and they were standing next to me with a bucket of water. My brother was always my mother's favorite, and I… Wow! I can't believe I just told you all that. I've never told anyone about my family before."

"It's okay," said Annie. "You know about my family already. Your family can't be any worse than mine."

They'd been walking for little more than an hour when they stepped onto a hard-beaten path. "Here we are," said Liam. "This is the road I was telling you about."

"It isn't much of a road. Are you sure it's not a deer trail?"

"It gets better farther on. I told you, I'm really good at tracking. Directions, too. I've been this way before with my father. It was years ago, but I doubt things have changed much."

"How far are we from Shimshee?" Annie asked.

"I'm not sure exactly where we are on the road, but there should be a sign up ahead with the distance posted on it."

It wasn't long before the road grew wider and had fewer rocks to trip them, and they soon emerged from the forest onto rolling farmland dotted with small, clear-water lakes. They didn't see any signs until they reached a crossroad and found two of them nailed to a tall post. The sign on the top was old and had two arrows, one pointing to the left and one to the right. The faded writing on the arrow that pointed to the left read *Kingdom of Shimshee, 12 miles*. The arrow pointing to the right read *Gallfield, 5 miles*. Under the arrows, someone had posted another sign that had been painted with fancy curlicues and flourishes. The sign read:

HEAR YE! HEAR YE! PRINCE ANDREAS OF
COREALIS IS HOLDING A CONTEST TO FIND
THE PERFECT PRINCESS TO BE HIS WIFE.
THE CONTEST WILL BE HELD AT THE
ROYAL CASTLE NEAR THE VILLAGE OF
GALLFIELD FOR THE NEXT TWO DAYS.
ALL UNMARRIED PRINCESSES MAY ENTER.

Annie was reading the sign for the third time when Liam pointed to the left. "Look, Shimshee is this way."

Annie sighed. "I know. We have to go find Digby. Too bad," she said as she turned to follow Liam.

CHAPTER 7

THERE WAS NOTHING to mark the border between the kingdom of Corealis and the kingdom of Shimshee except a white wooden stake standing at the edge of the road. A few nail holes at the top showed where a sign had once been posted.

"If I remember correctly, we're only three or four miles from the city of Kenless, where the royal castle is located," said Liam. "I think that's where we should start looking for Digby."

"Uh-huh," Annie replied. She had mixed emotions about finding Digby. Part of her wanted Digby to come back, kiss her sister, and have everyone wake up; the other part of her couldn't help but say—does it have to be Digby? If only Gwendolyn hadn't fallen for *him*!

Annie was still thinking about how much she couldn't stand Digby when she realized that she'd been smelling something new and different for some time. "What's that?" she asked, sniffing the air.

"We're near the ocean now," said Liam. "We should be able to see it soon."

"I've never seen the ocean," Annie said.

"Maybe we can go down to the beach before we leave."

"I'd love that," said Annie, "if there's time." She had never gone sightseeing before, and wouldn't have thought of it if Liam hadn't been with her, but having him there made the trip less of an ordeal, even when they didn't exchange a single word.

The next hill was higher than those around it. Annie's legs began to ache by the time they reached the top, but she knew right away that the climb had been worth it. The town that nestled at the foot of the hill surrounded a small port on three sides. Sailing ships rocked at their moorings while people scurried along the docks carrying heavy loads on and off the ships. Pennants flew over a castle that sat at the far end of the town keeping watch over the narrow streets. Just beyond the castle, a vast body of water spread out for as far as she could see, its undulating waves rushing toward the shore and lapping at the piers that jutted out from a gravel and dirt street.

Annie had never seen anything like it. The town itself seemed ordinary enough, but the ocean waves were almost hypnotic, and the limitless expanse was almost more than her mind could grasp. She stood there, open-mouthed and barely breathing, until Liam nudged her and said, "I've been thinking, when we get down there you should let me do the talking."

"Why?" Annie asked, dragging her gaze from the water to Liam. "I'm the princess. As my guard, you should just—"

"That's exactly why," Liam replied. "You're a princess. We're in a foreign kingdom without an adequate escort to keep you safe, so it's up to me. I'll do what I can, but you'll be safer if we don't let anyone except Digby know who you are. There's no saying what people would do if they knew the truth, so whatever you do, don't tell anyone else that you're a princess. You're still dressed as a boy. Let them think that that's what you are."

Annie shook her head. "My first visit to another kingdom and I'm going as a boy. It's not exactly how I pictured it."

"If we keep you safe now, someday you'll be able to go on a grand tour and do it with style."

"Maybe," said Annie. "But if I can't tell people who I am, how will I get an audience with Digby?"

"We'll go to the castle first," said Liam. "Someone there can tell us if Digby's at home. If he isn't, they might be able to tell us where he went."

A wall separated the town from the land beyond it. Though there were guards at the gates, none challenged Annie, Liam, or any of the other people entering on foot. Annie looked around her as she stepped into the shadows of the buildings that lined the narrow streets.

Shops and taverns vied for space with homes that couldn't be more than a small room wide. The second floors of many of the structures extended over the streets, blocking the sun so that it almost seemed as if night had come early. Unlit torches protruded from brackets on some of the buildings.

They were passing one such building when a door banged open in front of them and two men tossed a disheveled-looking figure into the street just feet from Annie and Liam. The man lay sprawled on the ground for a moment, then rolled over, got up, and staggered down the street, muttering to himself.

"Do you think he needs our help?" Annie asked, taking a step after the man. "He might be hurt. Those two men—"

Liam set his hand on her arm and pulled her back. "He doesn't need the kind of help we could give. That was a tavern," he said, pointing at a sign swinging overhead, "and I'm sure they had their reasons for throwing him out."

"Isn't it a little early for that?"

"Apparently not," said Liam.

Walking along the streets of the town, Annie thought that the people were as interesting as the buildings. She heard accents from many different kingdoms and saw clothes that were a jumble of all sorts of styles. Because it was obvious that she was paying more attention to the people than where she was going, Liam placed a hand on her shoulder and guided her around the unsavory puddles and piles of refuse that would never have been allowed to accumulate on the streets of Shelterhome.

Although Liam seemed to know where he was going, Annie soon lost all sense of direction. When she glanced up, hoping to see the castle, the buildings so completely blocked the view that they reached the castle entrance before she was even aware that they were close.

A long line of visitors hoping to gain access to the castle grounds waited for their turn to pass through the gate. When it was Liam and Annie's turn, Liam stepped forward and said to the guard, "We're here to see Prince Digby."

"Are you now?" the guard replied, letting his gaze wander up and down both Liam and Annie.

Annie tried not to blush, but the man didn't notice and had already turned his attention back to Liam.

"And why should we let boys like you in to see the prince?"

"Because we have urgent news about Princess Gwendolyn," Annie said, forgetting her agreement to let Liam do all the talking. "Prince Digby needs to hear it right away."

"Really?" sneered the guard. "And what would that be? If it's good enough, I'll see about letting you in."

"We can't just—," Annie began.

"Never mind," said Liam. "Come along, brother. This was a waste of time."

Annie was still protesting when Liam hustled her away from the gate and into the jostling crowd. "What are you doing?" she asked, trying to pull away from him. "I'm sure we could have convinced him to let us in!"

"Probably, but not to see Digby. You have a girl's voice. He was bound to realize the truth if you'd kept talking, and we'd both have been thrown in the dungeon as spies. They'd never believe a princess would come to the castle like this."

"Then how do you suggest we find Digby?"

"We'll ask someone else," said Liam. "There are always people ready to gossip about a royal family. Look for someone who likes to talk. Someone like…that man over there."

A short little man with a large belly had set up a stall near the end of the line of people waiting to go through the gate. The smell of hot grease wafted through the crowd, and more than one person was already munching the crispy pastry-wrapped meat pies he was selling. As another customer walked away from the stall, Liam approached the vendor.

"There's quite a crowd here today," Liam said, handing the man a coin. "Is it always like this?"

"Most days," the man replied. Wrapping a hot meat pie in a scrap of parchment, he dropped it in Liam's outstretched hand. "Some days it's a lot busier, especially when there's a beheading or when the troops come back from a skirmish. I can't keep up with the demand then."

"Or on holidays, when the royal family opens the gates to hand out food and such. There's never enough that's free, so people turn to Garvey and me since they're already in a holiday kind of mood," said the taller man in the next stall. "People with money always spend more on holidays."

"Does the royal family come out often? We were wondering if we'd see Prince Digby today," Liam said, glancing back toward the castle.

"You must not be from around here," said Garvey. "Everyone here knows about Digby. Where are you from?" he asked, raising an eyebrow.

"Treecrest," said Liam.

The taller man nodded as he skewered a tiny fried fish on a sharp stick. "Digby went there a few months back, didn't he? I remember hearing something about a princess."

"That's right," said his friend. "She's supposed to be a real looker. Have you ever seen her, or is she one of those prisses who never goes where she might get her dainty little shoes dirty?"

Annie opened her mouth to speak, but Liam pinched the back of her arm. "I've seen her," he told them, "and she's as beautiful as they say."

The man selling the fried fish shook his head. "She can't be any prettier than my wife."

"What are you talking about?" Garvey said, turning on him. "My backside is prettier than your wife!"

"How can you say that? She's your cousin!"

"Then I should know, shouldn't I? Why, just the other day my uncle said to me—"

"So what about Prince Digby?" Liam interjected before they really got distracted. "Does he come out of his castle very often?"

Garvey snorted. "Is he ever in it, do you mean?"

"He's not here right now," said the other man, reaching for another fried fish. "But if you wait around, you might see him sooner or later."

Garvey took a coin from a customer and nodded his thanks. "Later, if you ask me," he said, glancing at Liam. "He's probably at the Castle, like always."

"I thought you said he wasn't here," Liam said, looking confused.

The man selling fish shook his head. "Not this castle, boy. He means the Gray Castle Tavern. You can't miss it. The Castle is the prince's favorite. He's there more often than he's here. Now," he said, turning back to Garvey, "why would you say that about my wife when..."

As the two men resumed their argument, Annie and Liam slipped through the crowd and headed back into the town, splitting the cooling meat pie as they walked. "The Gray Castle was the tavern where that man was thrown out," Annie said, licking the grease from her lips as she glanced at Liam. "I remember the sign—a gray castle on a field of green. Digby might have been in there when we went past."

"Unfortunately," said Liam. "If that's the case, I hate to think what kind of shape he's going to be in when we catch up with him."

໕

When they found him, Digby was seated with two barmaids perched on his knees, watching bleary-eyed as the tavern keeper refilled his tankard. It was apparent from the expression on his face and the way he moved with exaggerated care that he had already been drinking for some time. The half-dozen men seated around him were even further gone than he was; one was snoring with his head on the table and two were arm-wrestling in spilled ale, laughing each time they slammed their arms down and splashed their faces.

No one paid any attention to the two newcomers until Liam took a seat near the prince. "I didn't give you permission to sit," Prince Digby said, and took a large gulp from his tankard. When he tried to set the tankard down, he hit the edge of the table and dumped most of the ale on one of the barmaids. She shrieked and hopped to her feet. Scrubbing at her clothes with the filthy rag she used to wipe the tables, she scurried from the room, leaving Digby and the other barmaid laughing.

"I can't talk to him when he's like this," Annie told Liam.

"I'll see what I can do."

Annie had never had to help a drunk get sober before,

but apparently Liam had, because he knew just what to try. He explained to the tavern keeper the kind of assistance he needed. The man refused to help until he heard how many coins he would be paid. Suddenly Liam had all the help he needed from the tavern keeper and two of Digby's less drunk friends. Digby seemed to think it was funny when Liam ordered a large mug of beef blood, stale ale, and a few even less savory ingredients. He didn't find it amusing, however, when the tavern keeper brought the concoction and the four men made Digby drink some. They were able to get nearly a third of it down the prince's throat before he knocked it out of their hands, declaring, "I'm not drinking that swill!"

"Then we'll try something else," said Liam, hauling Digby to his feet. The tavern keeper supported the prince's other side while Liam draped Digby's arm across his shoulders and walked him out the back door to the well used by all the buildings sharing the common open space. Annie watched from the doorway as they alternated dousing the protesting prince with bucket after bucket of ice-cold water and walking him between the buildings. By the time they let him sit on a bench, he was drenched and shivering, but didn't seem quite so drunk.

"We came to talk to you," Annie began. "It's about Gwendolyn."

"Do I know you?" he asked, peering at her through nearly closed lids.

Annie sighed. "It's me, Princess Annabelle. You know, Gwendolyn's sister."

"The plain one!" exclaimed Digby.

"She isn't plain," Liam said, thumping the prince on the back so that he nearly fell off the bench.

"Hey!" Digby exclaimed. He turned around to face Liam, standing behind him. "She's wearing pants and looks like a boy! What do you expect me to think? Although even when she's dressed like a princess, she still—"

Liam thumped Digby again. "The princess has something to say; listen to her."

The prince turned back to Annie. "What's this about? Is Gwendolyn here? I knew she'd pine away for me! After I kissed her in the garden she—"

"No, she's not here. We have a problem and it's up to you to fix it."

"What kind of problem?" Digby said, suddenly looking sly.

"I'm sure you've heard about the curse," Annie began. "Well, it's happened, despite all our efforts. Gwennie pricked her finger on a spinning wheel and will sleep until her true love kisses her. My mother insists that you're the one to do it, and she sent me to tell you so."

"Why did she send you? Why not a regular messenger?"

"Because everyone else is asleep," said Annie. "Apparently it was part of the curse."

"Why aren't you asleep, too?" asked Digby.

"Because the magic missed her, that's why," Liam said before Annie could respond. "So, are you going to do it or not?"

"I don't know," said Digby. "It doesn't sound safe..."

Liam's lip curled in disgust. "You're supposed to be a prince! If you're ever going to be king, you should start acting like one!"

"What do I get if I do kiss her?" Digby asked.

"You'll wake your true love from an unending sleep," said Annie.

"Uh-huh."

"You'll earn the gratitude of an entire kingdom."

"I really don't think—"

"You'll get to marry her."

"And?"

"And be king of Treecrest someday," Annie added, getting a bitter taste in her mouth when she said it.

"Now that's more like it!" Digby declared, jumping to his feet. "I'll go right now and—"

"Don't you think you should clean up and get your horse first?" asked Liam.

Digby looked down at his dripping tunic and nodded. "No sense going anywhere looking anything but my best," he said, then glanced at Annie and sneered. "Unlike some people, I care about appearances."

"I can tell," Annie said, glancing from Digby to the

tavern door. "Listen, you'll have to go on ahead without us. We have an errand to take care of first. We'll meet you there as soon as we can. If you get there before we do, don't try to get through the roses until I'm there to help you."

"If you get tired of waiting for us outside the castle, there's a nice inn you could visit in Shelterhome," Liam told the prince. "I've heard that The Linder Tree serves good, stout ale."

"I just hope it's good enough for my palate," said Digby. "I don't drink swill."

Annie glanced at Liam as they left the tavern and started toward the town gate. "Thank you for helping me talk to Digby. I've never tried to get a man sober before and wouldn't have known what to do if you hadn't been there to take care of it."

Liam swept her a playful bow. "I'm here to help however I can."

"Did you notice that Digby never once asked how Gwendolyn was doing? He doesn't care about her. All Digby cares about is Digby—and appearances, of course."

"You shouldn't listen to anything someone like Digby says, especially when they accuse you of being plain. You're not. In fact, I think you're really pretty." Liam glanced down at Annie. "Beldegard was wrong. You don't look anything like a boy and you're just as pretty as your sister. Prettier even. I should have taught him a lesson for insulting you like that."

Ordinarily Annie would have complained that she didn't like it when people lied, but Liam hadn't said it as if he were trying to flatter her. He actually sounded mad, the way she would if she'd heard someone state a blatant untruth. It surprised her how pleased that made her feel.

"So," he said before she could think of a reply, "what errand is so important that we have to do it now?"

"Mother wanted me to tell Digby about my sister, but I've been thinking... What if he really isn't the right prince for Gwennie? What if he goes back to the castle and kisses Gwennie and she still doesn't wake up? Then I'd have to get rid of Digby and find someone else. I'd have wasted all that time when I could have been finding the right prince."

Liam nodded. "That's true. So what do you want to do about it?"

"Go to Gallfield and see if I can still enter that contest! If I win, I'll ask that prince to go back with us. I'd feel better if we took more than one prince to see Gwennie."

CHAPTER 8

SHORTLY AFTER LEAVING THE CITY, they met a farmer whose wagon had lost a wheel. With Liam's help, the farmer got the wheel back on and was happy to give them a ride as far as the crossroads where the sign about the contest still fluttered in the breeze. As the farmer's wagon rumbled off, Annie hefted her satchel onto her shoulder, then paused a moment and set it on the ground.

"What are you doing?" Liam asked as she rummaged through the satchel.

"I think it's time I changed my clothes and started looking like a girl again." Pulling her rumpled gown from the sack, she shook it and sighed when she saw just how wrinkled it was. "It will have to do," she murmured to herself, then announced over her shoulder, "I'll be right back," as she started toward the woods.

Unlike most of her gowns, this one was simple

without fancy lacings or anything that Annie couldn't handle herself, so it took only a few minutes to change her clothes. When she returned to the road, Liam was lying on the grass with his eyes closed. "Wake up," Annie said, kicking the bottom of his shoe.

Liam opened his eyes partway. "I wasn't asleep. I was just resting my eyes. You didn't take nearly as long as I expected. It takes my mother at least an hour to change her gown. Let's go," he said, getting to his feet. "We don't have time to waste."

Annie took her sack from his outstretched hand and tried to match her steps to his as he set off down the road. Every so often she cast a curious glance his way. He'd let slip little things about himself now and then that were just enough to make her realize how much she didn't know. His mother took a while to dress, which might mean that his family had money. His father liked weapons and had given him a sword when he was young. That made her think his father was either a knight or a sword smith. The only other thing she knew about him was that he didn't get along with either his mother or his brother.

Annie liked knowing even that little bit about him. She thought of him as a friend rather than a guard now, and she suspected that he felt the same way. After all, he no longer called her Your Highness, or spoke to her with the same deference that he had used in the castle. She didn't mind, although her parents and sister would have taken great exception to his familiarity. Circumstances had changed, however, and although she might need a guard, she needed a friend even more.

If only he could be more than that, Annie thought, and was surprised that she had thought it. She gave herself a mental shake. It would be easy to fall in love with someone like Liam. He was sweet and considerate and actually listened when she spoke. Because she could be herself around him, she enjoyed his company more than that of any other man she'd ever known. He was handsome in a uniquely Liam sort of way, and she loved the way his eyes crinkled at the corners when he smiled. She could see herself married to someone like him ... only it couldn't *be* Liam. He was a commoner, and her parents would never give their approval. Her parents' wishes had always been so important to her that she couldn't disregard them now, not even when Liam reached for her hand to help her over a ditch where part of the road had washed away and she felt reluctant to let go afterward.

"We must be getting close to Gallfield," Liam said as they reached the highest point on the narrow bridge they were crossing and saw that the road beyond was in better repair.

"Uh, right," Annie said, glad that Liam couldn't know what she'd been thinking.

They were entering Gallfield when they saw the first hint that a celebration was in progress. The town had gone to great trouble to clean the streets, scrubbing down the cobblestones and placing tubs of flowers in front of the homes and shops. The streets were deserted, however, and they didn't see anyone until a girl came running out of a cottage, carrying a basket.

"Pardon me," called Liam, "but do you know where the contest is being held?"

The girl, who was only a few years younger than Annie, stopped and waited for them to catch up to her. Smiling and pink-cheeked, the girl was so excited that the words seemed to bubble out of her. "On the castle grounds, which is only fitting, wouldn't you say? We're all thrilled to pieces! Prince Andreas is finally going to get married. We've been hoping for ages that he'd pick a bride soon, but he's never been able to find the right one. I'm Maud, by the way. My mum works in the castle kitchen, and she knows all about the prince. Do you know that he's almost twenty years old? He's very particular, everyone says so. But six princesses have come to try for his hand. One of them is bound to be the right one. I came home to get my dad and me a bite to eat and I'm on my way back there now, so I'd be happy to show you the way. You can see it now. Oh, look! They're getting ready for the next contest."

Annie hurried forward, anxious to see what she was about to get herself into. She could see the castle, rising above the trees. It wasn't very big as castles went, but it was well built and fairly pretty, with each of its five towers flying colorful pennants. She could hear the crowd now, and as she drew closer she saw people dressed in their best clothes watching from the perimeter of a large clearing.

"Who's in charge of the contest?" Annie asked the girl.

"That would be Lord Penbroken. That's him, over there by that table."

A group of more formally dressed people were standing near a trestle table that had been set up at the end of the clearing. An elderly man was talking to a group of pretty young women, who Annie assumed were the princesses. Although every one was lovely in her own way, none of them were nearly as beautiful as Gwendolyn.

A horse whinnied and Annie turned to see grooms escorting a small herd toward the princesses. As each horse was brought up, a princess left the group and walked into the clearing with the horse and groom. It wasn't long before Lord Penbroken was by himself. When Annie approached him, the elderly man barely spared her a glance. "Excuse me," she said, "but can you tell me if it's too late to enter your contest?"

Lord Penbroken looked irritated when he turned to face her. "This contest is for princesses only. If you happen to have a princess in your entourage," he said, giving her a condescending smirk, "she may enter."

Annie brushed back a lock of her hair. She had neither bathed nor washed her hair in days, and she knew she must look terrible, but there was no time now to do anything about it. "I'm glad to hear that," she told the elderly man. "I'd like to sign up."

"*You're* a princess?" asked Lord Penbroken.

Annie nodded. "I'm Princess Annabelle of the kingdom of Treecrest, come to enter your contest. I can give you a list of all my ancestors if that would help."

Lord Penbroken looked a little dazed. "I don't see how—"

"Let her enter the contest, Penzi," said a tall young man who had arrived while they were talking. "The more the merrier, I always say."

"Yes, Your Highness," murmured Lord Penbroken.

"You must be Prince Andreas," said Annie, curtseying as one would to an equal. "I'm Princess Annabelle, but my friends call me Annie."

The prince smiled, displaying a set of white teeth made perfect by magic. "Then by all means, Annie it will be."

"Do you need to hear my ancestry?" she said, turning to Lord Penbroken.

The elderly man glanced at the other princesses and shook his head. "No, no, there isn't time for that now. You may enter, provided you know that there will be dire consequences if you've lied to us and you aren't really a princess. You've missed the first part of the contest, but we'll talk about that later. Right now we'll have to see about getting you a horse."

"Excuse me," said Prince Andreas as he reached for Annie's hand and raised it to his lips. She noticed that his fingers grew stubbier in the few seconds he touched her. "They've brought out my mount. I'll see you during the contest, Annie."

As the prince walked out into the clearing and Lord Penbroken turned away to talk to a groom, Annie discovered that Liam had followed her. "He's quite charming," she said in a quiet voice. "I think he'd do very well for Gwendolyn."

"Huh," said Liam. "Are you sure you're still thinking about your sister?"

Annie gave him a sharp look. She couldn't help it if she'd been wondering what it would be like to be entering the contest for herself rather than her sister, just as she couldn't help feeling guilty that she could think such things when her family needed her so. "What is that supposed to mean?" she asked Liam. "Finding a prince for Gwennie is the whole reason we're here."

"I know. I just want you to keep that in mind. You should also keep in mind that no prince appreciates being deceived."

"So is it true? Are you a real princess?" asked Maud, pushing through the crowd around them. "Because I have a lot of friends who would have loved to do what you just did, only none of them have the nerve. Everyone around here knows them too well, too, but a stranger like you—"

"It's true," Liam told her. "She really is a princess."

"It's lucky they let you start now," said Maud. "Seeing that they already had the first contest."

"Mmm," Annie murmured. She was watching the princesses pet the horses as if the animals were big dogs. Every one of the girls was lovely, delicate, and carried herself as gracefully as Gwennie. Depending on what the contests were, Annie could either embarrass herself by how terrible she was in comparison, or . . .

"What was the first contest?" Annie asked.

"Poetry," said Maud.

Annie grimaced. "I'm glad I missed it then. I hate poetry. The best I can do is a lousy limerick."

"Princess Sarinda won it. That's her, over there in the pink gown. The one who just fell off her horse."

The princess in pink was lying on the ground, having been boosted onto the horse's back and fallen off the other side. Another princess with red hair and a pale green gown had a grim expression on her face as she dug her legs into the horse's sides to keep from falling off. Of the six princesses, only two had control of their horses.

"So the next contest is horseback riding?" said Annie. "But none of those horses are saddled. Most princesses ride sidesaddle."

Maud leaned close enough to whisper into Annie's ear. "Prince Andreas wants a wife who can keep up with him, no matter what."

A princess with dark brown ringlets lurched onto

her horse's back and grabbed hold of its mane instead of the reins. "I see," said Annie, thinking that she might have a chance after all.

"It seems they've found a horse for you to ride," Liam said, gesturing toward the clearing.

Annie was pleased to see that they had brought her a pretty little palomino mare with a dance to her step. She had learned to appreciate horses from her friends in the stables and knew a good horse when she saw one. Leaving Liam with Maud, Annie crossed the grassy meadow. After taking a moment to pat the mare's neck, Annie let the groom give her a hand up, deftly climbing onto the horse's back. Taking the reins from his hands, she turned the horse toward where Prince Andreas was waiting. Some of the princesses were already there, facing the prince in a straggly row, but it took a few more minutes and the help of their grooms before the rest of the contestants joined them.

"I'd like you all to meet Princess Annabelle, who will be joining our contest," the prince said when everyone was ready. "I'm sure you'll all do your utmost to make her welcome." The six princesses turned and gave her nasty looks, but the prince didn't seem to notice. "The rules of this contest are simple," he continued. "We will race around this field until I decide it's time to stop. Whoever can keep up with me wins. Any questions? Yes, Princess Daphne?"

"This horse doesn't like me," said the princess with

the dark brown curls. "Would it be possible to get a different one?"

"I want the one she's on," said Sarinda, pointing at Annie. "That horse is better behaved. It isn't fair that she gets the good one when she just got here."

"Now, now, ladies, these horses are all well behaved or they wouldn't be in my stable. If there aren't any *real* questions…Good. When Lord Penbroken counts to three, we start." Raising his hand, the prince gave a signal.

"One, two, three!" shouted Lord Penbroken.

Prince Andreas's horse took off like a shot, leaving the other horses to snort at the dust cloud he'd left behind. Princess Sarinda kicked her horse, which reared, dumping her on the ground. Daphne patted her horse and asked it to move, but it refused to budge. While two other princesses milled around, trying to get their horses to go where they wanted them to, Annie and a princess in a lavender gown raced down the field after the prince.

Annie loved the sense of freedom riding bareback gave her. She'd often gone out into the fields where the horses were pastured, thrown a rope around a horse's neck, and raced with the stable boys until it was time for them to return to work, and she to her duties as a princess. Annie had won more often than not, although she hadn't had the time to do it of late. Now, racing with Prince Andreas, she let herself go in a way she never would have with anyone but her friends. It was fun, it was exhilarating, and she hoped he wouldn't tire of it soon and declare that it was over.

She was laughing from excitement, her hair whipping in the wind behind her, when the princess in lavender screamed and galloped past straight into the woods instead of following the curve of the field. "Princess Clotilde!" shouted a rider stationed at the edge of the woods. Seeing that the rider was already trying to stop the runaway horse, Annie urged her horse to go faster in an effort to catch up with Andreas. The prince turned his head to look back, grinning when he saw that Annie was gaining ground.

Together, Annie and Prince Andreas raced around the field once, twice, three times. Although Annie could have passed him, she remembered that Maud had said the prince wanted a princess who could keep up with him, which wasn't at all the same as saying that he wanted one who could beat him. The palomino mare wanted to run faster, but Annie held her back, giving her a silent apology.

After two more circuits around the field, Andreas held up his hand and slowed his horse to a walk. They returned to Lord Penbroken amid the cheers and applause of the watching crowd, but Annie noticed that none of the other princesses had waited for the end of the race and had already returned to the castle. While Lord Penbroken announced that Princess Annabelle of Treecrest was the winner of the contest, Andreas slipped from his horse and crossed to Annie's, where he offered to help her down.

"Very nicely done," said the prince, and kissed the back of her hand.

"Thank you, Your Majesty," said Annie, curtseying. She couldn't help adding, "It was fun!" which earned her a guffaw from the prince.

"I'll see you at the ball tonight."

Annie looked dismayed. "There's a ball? But I don't have a gown to wear."

"Don't worry about that," said Prince Andreas. "Once my mother hears that you won this contest, she'll make sure you have twenty gowns to choose from!"

CHAPTER 9

ANNIE WAS SHOWN TO A ROOM where she could freshen up. There she found a selection of gowns and a stern-looking lady-in-waiting named Lady Hillary. A long, narrow, hot water–filled wash tub awaited her as well. This alone was a luxury she hadn't hoped to find, but she was even happier when she discovered a piece of soap that smelled of violets.

Before Annie handed her dirty clothes to Lady Hillary, she made the older woman promise that they would be washed and hung in front of a fire to dry so they'd be ready for her to wear after the ball. The lady-in-waiting bundled up the soiled clothes while Annie slipped into the tub and sighed as the heat drew the ache from her muscles. She took her time washing her hair and body with the violet soap, reveling in the scent of flowers and the feeling of finally being clean again.

Annie was putting on a cream-colored gown

embroidered with violets when she thought to ask the lady-in-waiting for something to eat. To her surprise, Lady Hillary shook her head and said, "I wouldn't advise it. You'll be dining after the dance. It wouldn't hurt you to wait until then. I wouldn't suggest eating right before you engage in vigorous exercise."

"What kind of dance is it?" Annie asked. "Is it part of the contest?"

"I can't say," Lady Hillary replied in a way that Annie took to mean yes.

Annie nodded. "I see. Then I want to look my very best. Do you think you could find me some violets for my hair?"

For the first time since they met, the woman smiled. "I'm sure I can find something," she said, and hurried out of the room.

Annie sank back into the warm water and sighed. She hadn't seen Liam since the race, but she found herself wishing that she could talk to him. It occurred to her that it was odd, not just because he was a guard, but because she liked how open and honest he was with her, and how he treated her like an equal, which was the very thing her family would have hated about him.

She was still thinking about Liam when the lady-in-waiting returned with a nosegay of violets and the news that the ball would be starting soon. After tucking the flowers in Annie's hair, Lady Hillary escorted her through the castle to the Great Hall, where she left her with the other princesses.

"Look who's here," said the princess named Sarinda. The musicians were playing soft music as more people entered the room, but even so she had to speak up to be heard. "It's the princess from...Where did you claim to be from?"

"Treecrest," said Annie, pretending that the other girls weren't looking at her as if they'd like to poison her food.

"The princess from Treecrest is reputed to be very beautiful," said Daphne. "You can't possibly be her. You're not beautiful, or even pretty."

Annie kept a bright smile plastered on her face. No matter how often she'd been spoken to like this, she'd never gotten used to it. "You're talking about my sister, Gwendolyn. She's the most beautiful princess in the world, present company included."

Daphne turned to the other princesses. "It's no wonder she entered the contest. Ordinarily no prince would ever notice her. Andreas's contest is unique in that it has nothing to do with beauty."

"Not so far," Sarinda said. "We don't know what the rest of the contests will be." She turned to Annie and told her in an icy voice, "Don't assume you're going to win the prince just because you won that stupid riding contest."

Daphne sighed. "I wish they would tell us what the contests will be so we could prepare."

"That's probably why they haven't," said Sarinda.

"Actually—," Annie began.

"Shh!" Daphne said. "Prince Andreas approaches!"

Annie smiled to herself as the other princesses began to pat their hair and straighten their gowns.

"Your Highnesses," said the prince, bowing to them all.

"You look very handsome, Your Grace," said Sarinda.

"And you all look lovely," he replied. "Princess Daphne, I believe this is our dance."

Even as Prince Andreas led Daphne to the middle of the room, Annie knew it wasn't going to be a traditional kind of dance. Most dances were done in lines with multiple couples, but no one else made a move to join them. Annie laughed to herself when the music began and she saw the surprised look on the princess's face. Daphne's expression turned to one of dismay when the prince put one hand on her back and took her hand with the other. Andreas pushed and pulled the princess around the room, roughly in time with the music. Within the first few minutes, he stepped on Daphne's feet, shoved her so fast that she nearly tripped, and twirled her until she looked ill. It wasn't until he twirled her into a wall with a loud thud and she walked away rubbing her head that she finally asked to sit down. Instead of looking sorry, the prince looked smug.

Princess Clotilde was his next partner. The music

was a lively country jig, one that Annie knew well, but the princess acted as if she'd never heard it. Although she tried to follow Andreas's steps, he moved too quickly and she was unable to avoid his feet when he stomped on her dainty slippers. The second time he stepped on her foot, she excused herself and hobbled to the side of the room.

Andreas whispered into the ear of his next partner as they danced. Annie could see the princess becoming more and more uncomfortable. Her eyes grew wide as he talked, and she blushed a deep shade of pink almost as vivid as her flame-colored hair. The prince seemed to be enjoying himself, however, and he smiled broadly when she abruptly let go of his hand, slapped his face, and ran from the Hall. Whatever he had said to that princess, Annie resolved that she would take the conversation in a different direction.

When Andreas raised his hand to stop the music, Annie followed him to the table set up against the wall. There was an odd assortment of food, with bowls of garlic cloves and small red onions placed beside dainty pastries and sweetmeats. Annie hadn't eaten since she shared the vendor's meat pie with Liam, and would have loved to have helped herself, but she watched when Andreas took a handful of small onions and garlic cloves and ate them as if they were candy. No one was watching when Annie popped garlic and onions into her mouth, too.

The music was just beginning when Annie returned

to watch Prince Andreas. He didn't even have to talk to his next partner before she made a terrible face—one whiff of his breath was enough. His wild steps and oniony garlic breath soon had her looking queasy and running from the Hall.

Annie thought the whole thing was funny and was laughing behind her hand when she noticed the last two princesses glaring at her. "Why are you laughing?" asked Sarinda. "You won't do any better than they have."

"We'll see," said Annie as Prince Andreas came to claim a partner.

The next piece of music was another lively one. The prince twirled his partner around and around until she was so dizzy that she couldn't stand, and collapsed in a heap when he let go of her hand.

"I'm the best dancer in my kingdom," Sarinda muttered under her breath, "but I can't dance like that! He isn't really dancing. He's playing some silly game."

"Exactly," said Annie as the prince escorted Sarinda onto the dance floor. "And the winner will be the one who plays along."

The prince's dancing was even wilder with Sarinda than it had been with the others. She didn't fall when he twirled her, and skipped nimbly aside when he tried to stomp on her feet, but when he danced her toward the raised dais at the end of the Hall and hopped up the two steps onto it, she faltered and nearly let go of his hand. Her face was flushed when she hopped up beside him—

then up, down, up, down…She tried to follow him as he hopped on and off the dais, but when he finally hopped down and started to dance across the floor again, her legs were so wobbly that they couldn't hold her, and she staggered into a courtier watching from the side, nearly knocking him down.

The music started up again as Prince Andreas took Annie's hand. It was a piece that had been played earlier, so Annie was ready when he tried to twirl her into the wall; she jumped out of the way so that he nearly bumped into it himself. When he tried to stomp on her feet, she skipped aside. Annie thought that she might have won when the first dance ended and she was still on her feet, but Prince Andreas wasn't finished yet.

The second dance was one of the strange, slow ones. "It's a new style of dance popular in the southern kingdoms," Andreas said, pulling her close. Because she'd held his hand for so long, she could clearly see what he looked like without magic. He wasn't handsome, but he had a nice face with the look of a mischievous boy.

When Andreas gazed into her eyes and blew a puff of oniony garlic breath in Annie's face, she blew her own garlicky onion breath back at him. He snorted and looked surprised, but a moment later he was laughing. "Very good, Annie," he whispered into her ear. "You're smarter than the rest as well as an excellent dancer. You know, I'd really like to get to know you better. What do you say we leave the Hall and—"

"Go play a game of chess!" Annie suggested. "Or checkers if you'd prefer. I know a lot of card games, too, and a page taught me an interesting game using dice."

"Really?" said the prince, looking intrigued. "My favorite game uses small round stones and dice. I could show you that one if you'd like."

"That would be wonderful!" said Annie.

The music pulled them apart for a moment, and when it brought them back together the prince tried to take charge of the conversation again. His eyes were smoldering when he looked into hers, and he said, "I know a great place where we could go to be alone and—"

"The stable, right?" said Annie. "That horse you were riding was magnificent. Do you breed horses here in Corealis or do you buy them from a breeder?"

The prince's expression brightened. "Actually...," he began. The discussion about horses lasted until the dance was over; neither one noticed until the music stopped.

The next piece of music was a lively one and Annie was ready to be twirled when Andreas grinned and spun her around. Knowing that she would get dizzy if she spun too many times in one direction, she twirled in reverse back to the prince, only to be twirled again. When it was obvious that she wasn't getting dizzy, he danced her over to the dais and hopped up. Annie was ready for this move, too, and hopped up alongside him.

"I hear that they do this move in the southern

kingdoms, too," she said, and hopped into his arms so that he was supporting her weight.

Startled, the prince stumbled down from the dais and set her on her feet. "I believe I've heard about that move," he said, mopping his brow with a handkerchief that he pulled from his sleeve. "However, I'm not quite up to it." The prince's lips widened into a grin as he bent his knee into a courtly bow. "It appears that you have won this contest, Annie. Congratulations! I couldn't be happier!"

"Thank you, Your Highness," Annie said, curtseying.

"I must go tell my parents. They'll be ecstatic."

The prince hurried off into the crowd. A moment later Liam appeared, looking handsomer than ever in a clean set of clothes. "So you won another one," he grumbled.

"Two down," she said. "I wonder how many there are to go."

"I saw the way Andreas has been looking at you. Have you told him that you're doing this for your sister and not for yourself?"

"Not yet. I can't tell him during the contest or he'll disqualify me."

"And if you win, what would keep him from disqualifying you then?"

"My charm and good looks?" Annie said, giving him her warmest smile.

"That wouldn't work on *him*," Liam muttered under his breath as he turned away. He disappeared into the crowd lining the Great Hall as servants returned the tables and benches to their usual places. Only five princesses were ushered to the table that they were to share with Prince Andreas.

"Where are the others?" Annie asked Daphne as they took their seats across from the prince.

"They're indisposed," Daphne replied, glancing at Andreas.

"Lorelei is resting with a cold compress on her head and Bluebell is sick to her stomach," whispered Sarinda, who was sitting on Annie's other side.

"After all the exercise we've had today, I'm famished," said the prince, eyeing a steaming platter of roast goose. "I hope you've brought your appetites with you, ladies."

"Everything looks delicious," Annie replied. "I'm famished, too!"

"She's so common," she heard one of the princesses whisper to another.

Although the other princesses turned up their noses at the heartier fare, preferring to nibble quail's eggs and a soufflé of hummingbird tongues, Annie had a large helping of oxtail soup, then heaped her plate high with roast goose, venison, and blood sausage. She ate everything that the prince ate, including the smelly cheese that no one else touched. Annie had to force herself to eat slowly, but she couldn't make herself pick at the food the way the other princesses did.

After chewing her last bite and sipping her last sip,

Annie glanced up to see Andreas watching her with approval. "I like a girl with a hearty appetite," he said. "And now I have an announcement to make." Pushing his seat back, the prince strode to the front of the room and onto the dais.

Sarinda leaned forward to whisper past Annie to Daphne. They both looked a little less lovely than they had before sitting on either side of Annie, but neither one seemed to be aware of it. "He's probably going to announce the next contest," said Sarinda. "What do you suppose it is this time?"

"Whatever it might be, I hope we can sit down for it," Daphne replied. "My foot still pains me where Andreas tromped on it."

The room grew quiet as Prince Andreas joined his parents. "I'm sure you'll be happy to hear that I've made my decision," he announced. "We have a winner of the contest, so there's no need to look any further."

Sarinda's breath hissed out of her, Daphne bit back a sob, and the other princesses began to whisper among themselves.

"That's wonderful," said his mother, clapping her hands and beaming.

His father declared in a loud voice, "It's about time! Who is she, lad? Which of these lovely ladies has finally stolen your heart?"

"Princess Annabelle, from the kingdom of Treecrest! Annie, would you please join me?"

Annie hadn't expected to feel a pang of guilt as she rose from her seat and approached the dais. She had entered the contest hoping to find a prince for Gwennie, not herself. It really hadn't occurred to her that she had entered it under false pretenses, even though Liam kept trying to tell her that she had, but seeing the prince's radiant face made her realize just how unfair she'd been.

Clearly Andreas was looking for a wife who knew how to do the kinds of things that he enjoyed and would enjoy doing them with him. He was a robust, enthusiastic kind of person who didn't do anything halfway, and he wanted a wife who was the same. Magic had made all of the other princesses appear close to perfect, only it was someone else's idea of perfection, not Andreas's. The magically enhanced princesses were lovely and probably accomplished in the gentler arts, but not every prince wanted a wife who could look pretty while she embroidered. These girls would never dance the kind of dances Andreas liked, ride the way he rode, or share his interests. And if he married Gwennie, that was exactly what he would get.

"I don't know what to say," Annie said as the prince took her hand in his.

"What about the other contests?" Sarinda called in an angry voice. "We've only done two so far—the poetry contest and the riding contest."

"Four," said the prince. "The dancing contest and the eating contest count, too."

"There was an eating contest?" Daphne said, glancing down at her plate.

Sarinda's face was flushed when she stood up. "It still isn't fair. Princess Annabelle," she said, practically spitting out the name, "didn't have to make up a poem on a moment's notice the way the rest of us did."

"That's true," Andreas said. "Annie, you do need to make up a poem. It can be about anything at all."

"I'm not very good at poems," she whispered to the prince.

"What was that? We couldn't hear you!" called Sarinda.

"I'll try," said Annie. "If you'll give me just a moment."

"One minute," said Sarinda. "That's all we were given."

Annie thought about the contest and what the prince had really been after. She thought about how he'd feel when he learned the truth. Knowing that she had done only what she needed to didn't make her feel any better.

"I'm ready," said Annie, even as Sarinda opened her mouth again. "It's a limerick," she told the prince. "And not a very good one at that."

There once was a young prince who thought
That he'd find the princess he sought

125

By holding a contest
Where he could find the best
Wife who didn't have to be taught.

"Well done!" exclaimed Andreas. "I'd say that was good enough to win."

"There's a second part," Annie said, "if that's all right."

"Go ahead," said the prince.

Annie nodded and cleared her throat before beginning.

But the princess who garnered his hand
Hoped that he'd understand
That she'd entered to win
On behalf of her kin
And not for herself as he'd planned.

There was a moment of silence, then Andreas began to applaud. "Excellent!" he declared. "Even better than the first part. Although I must admit that you had me going there for a moment. I thought you meant that you—"

"Can I talk to you for a moment?" asked Annie. "Alone?"

"Certainly," he said, his smile fading. "Is something wrong?"

Annie felt terrible that she had to disappoint Andreas, and gave him a tremulous smile as she drew him into the corridor. She liked the prince and enjoyed his company. He was a more genuine person than most nobility, and she wouldn't have minded marrying him herself if only they'd met under other circumstances.

"Actually," she said, "something is wrong and I was hoping you could help. My sister is the victim of a terrible curse. She's asleep and will stay that way until her true love kisses her on the lips. I'm looking for a prince to kiss her and wake her up, and I was hoping that prince would be you."

Andreas frowned. "If you didn't want to marry me, you shouldn't have entered the contest."

"It isn't that I wouldn't like to marry you, but my sister, Gwendolyn—"

"Princess Gwendolyn? Isn't she supposed to be the most beautiful princess in all the kingdoms?"

"I understand how angry you must be with me, but Gwennie needs you and—"

"All she needs is one kiss? Then what happens, I mean, after I kiss her and she wakes up?"

"Why, it would mean that you were her true love, so I suppose you would get married and—"

"*I* would marry Princess Gwendolyn? The most beautiful princess in all the kingdoms?"

"Yes, and I know that wasn't what you had in mind, but—"

"No, no! I'd be happy to help. When do we leave? I

can be ready in twenty minutes. Make that thirty—I really should tell my parents that I'm going."

"You mean you're all right with this? You aren't angry that I deceived you?"

"Ordinarily, I would be furious, but this is Gwendolyn that you're talking about. I've heard so many stories . . . It is true what they say about her, isn't it?"

"Oh, yes, she is everything they say," Annie said, not sure how she felt about his reaction. It helped that he was so willing to go with her, but he didn't have to seem so eager to give her up for someone else, even if it was what she wanted. "There's no need to rush. Tomorrow morning will be soon enough."

"Marvelous!" said the prince. "At last I will meet my bride-to-be. There is one thing, though. If I don't get to marry Gwendolyn, can I still marry you?"

Annie looked incredulous. Maybe Andreas wasn't quite as great as she'd thought he was. "I don't think it would work that way," she said, shaking her head. When she got married, she wanted it to be to someone who considered her his first and only choice, not his consolation prize.

"Too bad," Andreas said, bending over to kiss her hand. "I really like you, Annie."

"What a numbskull," Liam said in her ear as Andreas returned to the Great Hall. "The most beautiful princess in all the kingdoms! She's nothing compared to you. The idiot doesn't have a clue as to what he just gave up."

"You're not saying that just to make me feel better, are you?" Annie asked.

"Me? Never!" Liam replied.

Annie looked into his eyes and was happy to see that he looked genuinely taken aback. "I'm glad to hear that," she said, surprised by just how much better she felt.

CHAPTER 10

ALTHOUGH BOTH ANNIE AND LIAM were ready to leave early the next morning, they had to wait for Prince Andreas, who was still sleeping. Annie wanted to go wake him, but when she asked Lady Hillary for the location of his room, the lady-in-waiting looked shocked and told her that it wasn't proper. Not knowing who else to ask, Annie waited until Andreas finally sent for her, saying that he was ready to go and that he was providing horses for Annie and her guard. The horses did help Annie's bad mood, but shortly after they crossed over the boundary between Corealis and Treecrest, Andreas insisted that they stop to eat at a village inn they were passing.

"We only just started our journey!" said Annie. "We've been on the road for less than an hour!"

"We wanted an early start, so I didn't eat before

we left," said the prince as he swung his leg over his horse's back and dismounted.

"That was an early start?" Annie said as Andreas disappeared into the inn.

Liam shrugged. "You were the one who wanted him to come along."

"Yes," said Annie, "but I didn't expect him to be so slow. Let's hope he isn't too hungry and we can get back on the road soon."

When they stepped through the door, they found Andreas seated at a table already eating a slab of roast beef and a hearty chunk of bread. "Have a seat," he said, waving his hand at the bench across from him. "You too," he told Liam. "I don't stand on ceremony when I'm traveling."

Liam looked annoyed when he sat down, but Annie was worried. She'd been thinking about the curse again, and she still didn't know what the hundred years part really meant. Did Gwennie have to sleep for one hundred years, at which time a prince would automatically come to find her, or could the prince come early, as Annie was trying to arrange, and still be able to wake her? Annie was doing her best by encouraging the princes to come, but what if that wasn't enough? What if Gwennie had to sleep the hundred years, too?

Annie was sipping a mug of lukewarm cider when a farmer came stomping into the inn, shedding clumps of dried mud from his boots. He took a seat a few tables from Annie and her companions, and scowled when the innkeeper's wife approached him.

"So, Dobs, have you gotten any more flowers?" she asked with a broad grin.

"No, I haven't!" said the farmer. "But if it ever happens again, I'm going to sell that danged beast! It'd be a shame, too. She's my best milker."

The innkeeper's wife laughed. "Maybe I'd buy her. My daughters and I like the flowers." She nodded toward a beautiful bouquet of tulips, daffodils, and irises filling a big copper kettle on a table in the center of the room.

After taking his order, the woman stopped by Annie's table to ask if they wanted anything else. "What was that all about?" asked Liam, gesturing toward the farmer.

"Farmer Dobs there had a cow get loose last week. He looked for her all over, but he couldn't find her and no one'd seen old Daisy. The very next day he heard a knock on his door and what did he see when he opened it? There was Daisy decked in flowers from head to tail. The fairy Sweetness N Light had led her there all the way from her garden using a daisy chain. Well, Dobs here had so many flowers that he didn't know what to do with them all, so he gave them to the ladies in the village. The ones he gave me are still blooming just as fresh as if they'd been picked yesterday."

"What else was I to do with them?" grumbled the old

farmer. "My wife died two years ago and I don't have any use for flowers."

As the innkeeper's wife teased Dobs, Annie leaned over to Liam and said, "Did you hear that? The fairy Sweetness N Light has her garden near here. She's the one who changed the nasty fairy's spell. I have to go talk to her if I can and ask about the curse."

"What about him?" Liam said, glancing at Andreas.

Annie sighed. Andreas had finished one plate of food and started on another. It didn't look as if he was going to finish eating anytime soon. "Would you mind going on without us?" she asked the prince. "There's a fairy I need to see. This shouldn't take long and we can meet you at my parents' castle."

"Don't worry about me," said Andreas around a mouthful of food. "I'll finish here in a few minutes and head out. I should reach the castle in a day or so."

"At the rate he's going," Liam muttered, "we could look for that fairy for days and still catch up with Andreas before he gets anywhere."

As they left they asked the innkeeper's wife if she knew where Sweetness N Light lived. "Everyone knows that," she said. Wiping her hands on her apron, she walked to the side of the street and pointed toward the forest. "Follow the road till it curves. You'll see a path there, leading to the trees. The Garden of Happiness is only a few miles into the woods. You can't miss it if you stay on the path. The fairies keep it nice, although hardly anyone uses it."

"I've never visited a fairy before," Annie said as she and Liam set off. "My parents wouldn't invite any to the castle after what happened to Gwennie, and they wouldn't let me go anywhere to see them."

"Most people don't want to have anything to do with fairies," said Liam. "They're very unpredictable. Even the good fairies can be more than a little crazy." He pointed at a swath of flowers planted beside the road. "That must be the path. I see what that woman meant about it being hard to miss."

Flowers grew in wild profusion on both sides of the path. Annie saw everything from tiny alyssum to sunflowers as tall as a man. At first the horses were more interested in nibbling the flowers than in walking down the path, but with a little encouragement they made their way into the cool shade of the forest.

Annie noticed that the sun-loving flowers gave way to the kind that thrived in the shade, but there were just as many blossoms as before. She was admiring the variety when she heard the sound of water overlaid with the whisper of magic. Glancing past the flowers on one side of the path, she saw a brook gurgling over brightly colored stones. Annie wasn't expecting the brook to speak to her.

"Where are you going?" it said in a sweetly musical voice. "Are you going to see the fairies? They'll be so happy if you are! Do you know them? I know them really well and I can tell you all about them. There's Sweetness

N Light, of course. She's so nice. You'll have to watch out for her though, because she ... Oh, look—a leaf! That tickles! The sunlight is so warm where the branches let it through. Isn't it a beautiful day? I do love the color of the sky, don't you? Want to hear a joke? How do you know the river is tired? Because he stays in his bed! Ooh! Look at that pretty pebble!"

"You were telling us about the fairies," Annie prompted.

"Was I?" said the brook. "What about them?"

"You said that we'd have to watch out for Sweetness N Light because ..."

"Because what? Do you know something I don't? Tell me! I love gossip. I hear it from the fairies all the time. They like to twiddle their toes in my water and talk about all sorts of things. Would you like to twiddle your toes in my water, too?"

"No thanks," said Annie. "We don't have time for twiddling."

"Don't encourage that stupid brook," Liam said under his breath, "or it will never stop talking. I can't stomach babbling brooks."

"It might be able to tell us something if it knows the fairies so well," Annie whispered back. "Tell me about Sweetness N Light," she said to the brook.

"She has pretty fingers. Oh, and she likes to sing. Do you like to sing? I do!"

Liam groaned when the brook began to sing a song

about pebbles. The brook was repeating it for the third time when they stepped into a big clearing. "Here we are!" the brook exclaimed.

"Finally!" said Liam.

"Would you look at that!" said Annie. She hadn't really known what to expect, but she never would have imagined anything like this. The trees of the forest had given way to a field that covered at least twenty acres. The entire garden was filled with a warm, rosy light that softened harsh edges and made everything look prettier than normal. Although the road ended at the entrance to the garden, the babbling brook continued on, meandering here and there past poppies and pansies, larkspurs and lilies. Every flower that Annie had ever seen or heard of grew in Sweetness N Light's garden, as well as many the princess had never known existed. The scent of so many flowers would have been delightful if it hadn't been a little overwhelming and made her head ache.

"I've never seen so many fairies in one place," Liam murmured.

Though they didn't see any human-sized fairies, there were flower fairies everywhere, flitting from blossom to blossom, dancing in the shade of hollyhocks, and holding hands while they skipped across the moss that grew at the edge of the brook. Many of them were laughing, but it was the singing that Annie noticed first. Their voices were so clear, true, and sweet that it sounded as if the flowers themselves had burst into song. A perky melody played continuously in the background, evidence of all the magic that was present.

"I think I'm going to be sick," Liam said. "This place is too cute for me. No wonder hardly anyone ever comes here. Let's leave as soon as we can."

"How do we find Sweetness N Light?" asked Annie. "Can big fairies turn into little ones like these? My parents always talked about her as if she were our size."

"She probably was a full-sized fairy. The more powerful fairies can be small or big, but I think most of the flower fairies are always tiny."

"Sweetness N Light's sitting by my sparkling pool!" said the babbling brook. "Follow me and I'll show you the way."

"This had better not take long," grumbled Liam.

Dismounting from their horses, they tied them to a tree at the edge of the garden and started on foot. With so many flowers covering the ground, it wasn't easy for Annie and Liam to find places to put their feet, so they ended up walking single-file along the narrow strip of moss that bordered the brook. They hadn't gone far when a group of flower fairies dressed in petal skirts and flower-bud hats gathered in front of them so they couldn't go any farther.

"Welcome to the Garden of Happiness!" they sang in a chorus.

"Come in and make yourselves comfortable," called one.

137

"Would you like something to eat?" cried another.

"Or drink?"

"Would you like to sit down?"

"Play a game?"

"Let's play a game," said Liam. "Hide-and-seek. You hide and we'll find you."

The fairies quivered with excitement. One dressed all in pink jumped up and down, shouting, "A game! We love games!"

"We're really good at hiding," said a fairy in a blue-bell cap.

"Uh, Liam," Annie began. "We really don't have time for—"

"I'll count to ten and you go hide," Liam told the fairies.

The fairies scattered as Liam counted. "...nine, ten. Come on," he said when he'd finished. "That should keep them busy for a while."

"That wasn't very nice," Annie whispered as they hurried along the bank.

"We're not here to be nice. I want to find that fairy and get out. I feel like I'm in one of those tales nursemaids tell to small children. I always hated stories like that."

After rounding a little knoll covered with nodding daisies, the brook ran downhill to a tiny waterfall that sounded like lilting laughter as the water cascaded into a small pond speckled with yellow water lilies. A fairy as tall as Annie sat at the edge of the pond holding a struggling badger in the shallow water while she scrubbed it with rose-scented soap. The fairy had hair the color of peach blossoms piled on top of her head in a pretty tumble of curls. When she glanced up, dimples flashed in her round, pink cheeks, and her robin's egg blue eyes crinkled at the corners.

"There you are," she said in a voice as sweet as honey when she saw Annie and Liam. "The brook told me that you were coming to see me. Welcome to my garden! Hold still, you dear creature," she told the badger. "After this you'll feel fresh and clean!"

Noticing how miserable the badger looked, Annie said, "Why are you washing it? Did it have a run-in with a skunk or something?"

"No, I just saw him in the forest and knew he needed it. I'm going to brush their teeth next," Sweetness N Light said, pointing at some frightened mice cowering in a cage made of dandelion stems.

"How ... sweet," said Liam, although Annie could tell from his expression that he was thinking something else entirely.

"Yes, isn't it?" the fairy said, smiling up at them. "I do so love to help others. It makes me happy when others are happy. Please sit down and make yourselves comfortable." They sat on the mossy bank. "Good. Now tell me, what can I do to make you happy?"

"Actually," said Annie. "I want to ask you about something you've done already. I'm Princess Annabelle. You helped my sister, Gwendolyn, once. It was at her chris-tening, about sixteen years ago," she added as the fairy continued to give her a blank look.

"I'm sorry," said the fairy. "I go to so many christenings..."

"It was here in Treecrest. The royal family—"

"Ouch!" said the fairy, jerking her finger back from the badger. "You bit me! None of the creatures I help ever bite me."

The badger had begun to growl deep in its throat. When Annie scooted away from it, she noticed that the mice were gnawing through the dandelion cage. The background melody of the magic was slightly out of tune.

"That weird light is fading," Liam whispered into her ear. "I think you're having an effect on her. You'd better hurry."

"You were there when the fairy Voracia cast a spell on my sister because she hadn't been invited to the christening," Annie told the fairy.

"Your sister wasn't invited to her own christening? How odd. Stop trying to bite me, you scamp!" she told the badger. The animal snarled and lunged for the fairy's hand; Sweetness N Light let go and sat back while it ran off. "If that's the way you're going to be, you can stay stinky!" she shouted after the badger, her voice no longer sweet.

"It was Voracia who hadn't been invited," said Annie. "She cast a spell to make my sister die if she pricked her finger on the spindle of a spinning wheel before she turned sixteen. Your gift changed the spell so that she would sleep instead of dying."

The fairy blew at a lock of hair that had come loose from the tumble of curls on top of her head and was hanging in front of her face. "I remember now," she said. "She was supposed to sleep for a hundred years and wake when her true love kissed her."

"That's right!" Annie said, relieved that the fairy remembered. "She touched a spindle and fell asleep along with everyone else in the castle. I'm trying to help her so they'll all wake up. I've already found some princes to kiss her, but I need to know about the hundred years part."

"I don't understand," said the fairy. "If everyone fell asleep, how come you're here? Shouldn't you be asleep, too? Oh, I get it. You weren't home when it happened. Then how did you find out?"

"I was home, but it didn't affect me," said Annie. "Another fairy cast a spell on me when I was a baby. Magic can't touch me and—"

Sweetness N Light drew back, a horrified look on her face. "You're that girl I've heard about! I didn't make the connection. No wonder that badger ... And look at my flowers! My morning glories are closing! Oh my! The mice are gone! And it took me so long to round them up. This is terrible! You have to leave right now."

"We'll leave as soon as you answer her questions," said Liam.

"Then hurry!" said the fairy as the last of the rosy hue disappeared from the meadow, leaving it looking quite ordinary.

"Does my sister have to wait a hundred years before she can wake up? If there's something I can do to wake my entire family, I'll do it. Just tell me what it is."

The fairy's flower petal skirt had dried out. When she plucked at one of the petals, it crumbled at her touch. "Only Voracia can end that part of the curse. My spell was tied to hers, you see. The exchange had to be of equal value—a hundred years and a true love's kiss instead of dying. If I recall correctly, the true love has to be a prince, too. Even so, unless the prince really is her true love, his kiss won't be worth a rat goblin's promise and she'll sleep forever. As to the hundred years... Voracia would have to waive that part for it to end early."

"Where can I find Voracia?" asked Annie over the sound of the waterfall. Instead of lilting laughter, it now sounded like rude catcalls and was already getting on her nerves.

"I'm sure *I* don't know," said the fairy. "West somewhere, I assume. Or is it south? There, that's all I can tell you. You have to leave now. And don't ever come back or I'll... Well, I can't turn you into anything, but that boy's a different story. Stay away from my garden or I'll turn him into something nasty."

142

"We're leaving," Annie said with a twist to her lips. "Thanks for your help."

The singing of the fairies that had sounded so sweet just minutes before now sounded off-key and the melody of the magic had become discordant. The fairies stopped singing altogether as Annie and Liam got to their feet, but the jarring melody of the magic continued.

Sweetness N Light frowned and looked around at the flower fairies. "Why did you stop singing? You know your singing makes me happy. Sing or I'll see that your flowers wilt!"

The flower fairies began to sing again, although with far less enthusiasm. Sweetness N Light was wearing a grim smile when Annie and Liam left her still sitting beside the pool.

"Did you notice that the brook isn't talking to us anymore?" said Annie as they followed it back toward the forest path. "Do you think it's because I've been around it so long, or that it's angry?"

Liam laughed. "I don't care why it's quiet. I'm just happy that it is!"

"At least someone's happy," said Annie. "I know I'd be a lot happier if Sweetness N Light had said the whole hundred years thing didn't matter. She wouldn't even have told us what she did if you hadn't said that we wouldn't leave until she answered my questions. If she'd wanted us to be happy, she would have given us some real help."

Liam snorted. "She says she likes to see other people being happy, but it seems to me that the only one whose happiness really matters to Sweetness N Light is her own."

They had almost reached the edge of the garden when the flower fairy in the bluebell cap landed on Liam's shoulder. "You didn't find us!" the fairy complained.

"You're right," said Liam. "I guess that just shows how good you are at hiding!"

"Oh!" said the fairy, looking pleased with himself.

As the fairy flew off to join his friends, Liam turned to Annie and said, "Did you see that? I can make people happy when I'm not even trying!"

"Good," she replied. "Then find Voracia and some more princes for me. I won't be truly happy until everything is back to normal again."

CHAPTER 11

"WHERE DO YOU WANT to go next?" asked Liam. His horse pawed at the ground, impatient at standing still. Annie's horse flicked its ears as if listening for her reply.

It was late afternoon, which meant that it was too early to stop for the night, but too late to get very far before nightfall. Annie peered up the road, using her hand to shade her eyes from the sun. "Where does this road go?"

"Southwest," said Liam. "If we stay on it long enough, we'll end up in Wryden."

"Sweetness N Light said that Voracia was either south or west, so I suppose southwest is a good compromise. We can ask if people have heard of her along the way."

Annie turned her horse to ride beside Liam and sighed with relief. The only sounds she heard were the clip-clop of their horses' hooves and the songbirds singing to their neighbors. She welcomed the quiet after the unceasing noise in Sweetness N Light's garden and was about to say so when Liam spoke up.

"Do you know what you're going to do once you find Voracia?"

"I have no idea," Annie replied. "But I'm sure something will come to me. It always does."

"In other words, you have no plan."

"None!" she said, and gave him her brightest smile.

Liam scowled and looked as if he wanted to argue, but Annie wasn't in the mood to discuss their options. Instead, she turned her attention to the countryside and let herself relax.

They rode through forest and open countryside without passing anyone and had just entered another, older wood where the trees were taller and the gloom deeper, when a horse whinnied and their two mounts answered. A minute later a man rode up behind them, hailing them as he approached. "Care for some company?" he said once he was close enough that he didn't have to shout. "This forest is no place to be alone after dark."

"Certainly," said Liam. "The more sword arms, the better. What brings you here at this time of day?"

"I'm Prince Cozwald of Bellaroost," the man replied, positioning his horse so that he rode beside Liam. Even in the gloom of the forest Annie could see that he was exceedingly handsome, with long, blond hair and chiseled features. "An ogre kidnapped the love of my life

146

and I'm going to rescue her. He's taken her to his castle just over the next hill."

"You're going by yourself?" Liam asked.

Prince Cozwald nodded. "I borrowed a magic ax from my father. He got it from his uncle, who got it from his father-in-law, who bought it from someone at a magic marketplace. It's supposed to kill an ogre with one swipe. I don't need anyone to go with me as long as I have this ax," he said, patting the weapon that was strapped to the back of his saddle.

They spoke together in low voices while the shadows deepened, but Annie began to feel uneasy and the young men soon stopped talking as they watched the forest around them. When the road angled uphill, Cozwald tightened his grip on his reins, making his horse prance with excitement.

"The castle is through the woods in that direction," the prince said as he peered into the gloom. "I was told that a road runs from this one to the castle gate. I'm going to camp in the woods tonight and enter the castle at dawn. Ogres are said to sleep during the day."

"Then we'll camp here, too, if that's all right with you, Your Highness," Liam said, turning to Annie.

"I think we should," she replied, certain that he'd called her Your Highness just to let Cozwald know that he wasn't the only royalty around. It had been days since Liam had called her anything but Annie. "I'm Princess Annabelle," she said, leaning forward so she could see past Liam to the prince. "I'm from the kingdom of Treecrest."

"I'm honored to make your acquaintance, Princess," said Cozwald, taking off his cap and inclining his head. "If I might ask the same question your friend asked me, why are you here at this time of day?"

"We're looking for a wicked fairy," said Liam. "We need her to undo a spell."

"Or at least change it," said Annie. "Then we have to find some more princes. I'd invite you, but you already have a lady love."

"What do you need the princes for?" asked Cozwald.

"I need to find my sister's true love. You might have heard of her. She's Princess Gwendolyn."

Cozwald nodded. "The most beautiful princess in all the kingdoms? Everyone has heard of her! Say, I have a cousin who is looking for a wife. He lives close to here. I can introduce you—after I rescue my princess, of course."

"That would be great!" said Annie.

Liam stopped his horse abruptly and pointed to the right, saying, "There's a road here."

Annie couldn't see anything except a gap in the underbrush, but she followed the prince when he turned his horse in that direction. Liam rode behind her with his sword in his hand. They'd ridden only a short distance into the woods when they smelled wood smoke from the castle's chimneys. It was dark when they dismounted and tied their horses' reins to branches. The men kept their weapons close at hand while they all collected wood, but when it came time to build the campfire, the prince kept watch while Liam made a ring of stones and lit the firewood inside it. He cooked their meager supper and was handing it out when he noticed that Cozwald had hung the ax from a loop on his belt.

"Is that your magic ax?" he said. "May I see it?" When the prince nodded and handed him the ax, Liam turned it over, inspecting the carving that covered the double-headed blade and the writing that ran up the handle. He hefted it in his hand and said, "It's nicely balanced, but are you sure it's magic? The blade is newer than the handle and looks as if it's never been tested. Annie, take a look at this."

Prince Cozwald looked uneasy. "My father said that his uncle swore—"

Annie shook her head when Liam tried to hand her the ax. "You'd better hold on to it," she told him. Tilting her head, she listened for the sound of some kind of magic, but there was nothing. "I'm sorry," she told the prince, "but if it ever held any magic, it's gone now."

"How would you know?" the prince said, snatching it from Liam's hand.

Annie sighed. "Because I can hear the presence of magic, and there isn't any in that ax. Either the magic has worn off or someone lied when they sold it to your uncle's brother's . . . whoever."

"That's not possible!" said the prince. "Wouldn't my father have known..."

"Why would he if no one had ever used it?" said Liam.

Cozwald plunked down beside the campfire and stared into the flames. "If the ax is no good, how will I kill the ogre and rescue my beloved?"

"I'll go with you," said Liam. "I've had a little experience with this kind of thing."

"You have?" said Annie. "When this is over, we have to talk. There's an awful lot I don't know about you."

Liam glanced at her, then looked away as if the thought made him uncomfortable. "Go ahead and eat. Our food is getting cold and we'll need our energy in the morning."

"You don't have to go with me," said the prince as he tucked the ax back into the loop on his belt. "I appreciate your offer, but this is my fight and I can't expect you to risk your life for a stranger."

"I said I'd go," said Liam. "You need my help and I'm willing to give it freely."

"And I'll go, too," said Annie. "After all, I need you to stay alive so you can introduce me to your cousin. We don't have much time, but the more princes I can take back with me, the more likely we are to take the right one."

"But...but...," the prince spluttered. "You're a princess. You can't go into an ogre's castle on purpose. No

150

princess would willingly spend even a moment in an ogre's company. You would be in great danger!"

"She'd be a big help," said Liam. "Believe me, I've seen what she can do. Besides, I don't want to leave her here by herself." Then he turned to Annie. "I think you'd be safer with me than alone in this forest at night. You'll have to listen to me, though, and stay back unless I say it's safe."

"I'll be good, I promise." Annie raised her hand as if she were pledging her fealty, then picked up the cup of broth Liam had given her and used it to soften the corner of a rock-hard crust of bread. She was about to take her first bite when a woman's shriek rent the silence of the forest.

Liam and Cozwald grabbed their swords and jumped to their feet, their eyes scanning the trees around them. "That must have been my beloved princess, Lizette!" said the prince. "She needs me now. I can't wait until morning to rescue her. Are you with me?" he asked Liam.

"We're both with you," said Annie, giving the crust of bread a regretful glance as she set it down.

It took them some time to reach the castle as they stumbled into trees and tripped over roots and fallen branches in the dark, but even so, Annie didn't regret her decision to go with them until Cozwald announced that they were going to scale the wall using the rope and weighted hook he'd brought.

"I don't know about this," she said, watching as the prince twirled the rope in a circle and tossed the hook up to the lowest window in one of the towers. The hook hit the ledge with a clang and fell back to land at their feet.

"I suppose I should have practiced," said the prince. Once again he twirled the rope over his head and let go. This time the hook held on to the window frame for a moment, but slipped off when Cozwald put his weight on it.

The hook barely missed hitting Liam when it fell. "Here's your problem," he said, picking it up to show the prince. "The tip of the hook is broken off."

Prince Cozwald looked stricken when he wailed, "How will we ever get in?"

"Leave that to me," said Liam. "I love rock climbing, and this shouldn't be very different."

After a quick smile in Annie's direction, he hung the hook on his belt and strode to the stone wall, where he raised his hands as high as he could reach. Annie was amazed when he grabbed hold of a tiny projection and pulled himself up the wall. With his toes fitting into small gaps between the stones and his fingers gripping edges so small that Annie couldn't even see them, Liam climbed the face of the tower. Disappearing through the window, he emerged a moment later without the hook.

"Good thinking," said Cozwald. Turning to Annie, he added, "He's fastened it to something. See, he's coming down now."

Liam held on to the rope and climbed down the wall even faster than he had climbed up. "Now it's my turn," said Cozwald. Grabbing hold of the rope, he climbed hand over hand up the wall with the agility of a squirrel.

"I'm not sure I can do that!" Annie said, turning to Liam.

"You won't have to. Here," he said, tying a loop in the rope. "When I reach the window, put your foot in this loop, wrap the rope around you like this, and I'll pull you up." He demonstrated what he meant until she was sure she could do it. When she was ready, he took the rope in his hand and peered up at the window. "You know, you really don't have to do this. I've fought ogres before without anyone's help."

"And did those ogres have magic?"

"Well, no, but—"

"Then I'm coming with you, because this one does. I can hear it from here. It's faint, but it's definitely there."

Liam grinned and bent down. Before she knew what he was doing, he had kissed her on the cheek and climbed the rope, leaving her surprised and breathless. "Ready?" he called softly from the window ledge.

"Give me a minute," she replied. Since the day the fairy had given her the gift that protected her from magic, no one had kissed Annie. Her parents had never come close enough, the servants wouldn't have dared, and it hadn't occurred to her friends. But now Liam, a guard without a drop of noble blood, had actually kissed her.

Annie touched her cheek and would have stood there savoring the warm feeling that left her shaky and confused if Cozwald hadn't called, "Hurry up or we'll leave you there!"

Sticking her foot in the loop, Annie wrapped the rope around her waist, then called back, "I'm ready!" A moment later she was gliding up the side of the tower, watching the window as it seemed to grow larger. When she reached the ledge, Liam helped her into the room. The moment she set foot on the floor, Cozwald rushed down the hall, his sword in his hand.

Liam shook his head. "The fool has no understanding of stealth. We should have tried to surprise the ogre, but there's no chance of that now. I want you to stay behind me," he said, glancing at Annie. "Just let me know when you sense magic." He took off running after Cozwald with his hand on the hilt of his sword.

Annie hitched up her skirts and dashed after him, muttering, "How can I tell him if he runs ahead?"

They found the prince waiting for them at a door at the end of the hall. He was about to open it when Liam put a hand on his arm and turned to Annie. "Does this door have any magic?" he asked her.

Annie shook her head. "Not that I can tell."

Tightening his grip on his sword, Cozwald shoved the door open and dashed inside. Torches flickered and burst into flame, illuminating the room that had been dark until he entered. A table and two chairs occupied

154

the center of the room. The remnants of someone's supper covered the table, the grease on the trenchers already congealed. Aside from a cat licking a platter, the room was unoccupied.

Annie followed the two young men into the room and paused to look around. It seemed innocent enough, although the floor was dirty and the sticky smears on the table showed that it hadn't been washed for a very long time. The room smelled musky, and she'd just decided that the smell was probably ogre when Cozwald opened the door opposite the one they had entered.

"Wait!" said Annie. She could hear a faint tune coming from the hallway—five notes playing over and over again. The tune was peppy and didn't sound like anything bad or evil, but any magic meant that they should be cautious. Cozwald didn't wait, however, and ran out the door, turning down the hallway that ran past it. Liam swore and ran after him. Annie took only a few steps before the door behind her burst open, although she couldn't recall closing it. She turned, expecting to see a horrible ogre, and was surprised when Cozwald and Liam ran into the room.

They looked stunned to see her. "How did you get ahead of us?" asked Cozwald.

"I asked you to stay behind me," Liam said.

"I did stay behind," said Annie.

There was a soft creak as the door began to close on its own. Cozwald turned so abruptly that his sword hit

155

one of the clay mugs on the table, knocking it to the floor, where it shattered with a crash.

Startled, the cat jumped off the table and ran out of the room before the door had closed all the way. "I tried to tell you that there's magic around," said Annie as the two young men headed for the opposite door.

"That cat was probably enchanted," said Cozwald.

"No, I don't think that was—," Annie began, but a loud shriek that seemed to come from everywhere made her stop and look around. The sound was fading away when someone laughed maniacally. Liam and the prince tore out the door.

This time when they disappeared, Annie didn't try to follow. She had noticed another door covered with the same wood paneling as the walls, as if it was meant to blend in. The floor in front of it was so scuffed, however, that she found it easily. She had started toward the door when Liam and Cozwald burst into the room.

The prince skidded to a stop when he saw her. "You did it again! How do you do that?"

"I haven't done anything," said Annie. "You're the ones who keep running through this room. Haven't you noticed that it's the same room every time?"

"She's right. Here's the mug you broke," Liam said, poking the shards with the toe of his boot.

"There's magic in that hallway," said Annie. "You'll never get anywhere if you go that way."

"Then how do we get out of here?" asked the prince.

"We could try the other door," Annie said.

The young men seemed confused as their gaze wandered around the room, passing over the hidden seams. "What other door?" asked Liam.

"This one," said Annie, reaching for the handle. The door opened easily, revealing a staircase going up.

"I told you she could help," Liam told Cozwald. "Let's try to be quieter this time. Although I don't know what good that will do us," he added under his breath. "We've already made more noise than a flock of harpies."

"Maybe I should go first," Annie suggested, stepping toward the stairwell.

Both young men rushed to stop her, but it was Liam who planted himself in front of the door. "You can't go first when we don't know what you'll find," he said.

"I know that there's magic there, too," said Annie. She pushed past him and up the stairs. It was plain from Liam's expression that he wanted to stop her, but wasn't sure if he should.

Annie could hear the whisper of magic even before she reached the top step. Before setting foot in the hallway, she paused to look both ways. The torches in the hallway at the top of the stairs were already lit. Benches flanked the half-dozen doors that led off to either side. The air was colder here, and smelled stale. Although there were no windows, a light breeze skittered down the hallway, twitching the bottom of a tapestry and dragging clumps of black dog fur that caught at the legs of the benches and puddled in the corners.

"There's magic, but I don't know what it is yet," Annie told Liam in a soft voice.

"We don't have time for this," said Prince Cozwald, pushing past Liam and Annie. "My Lizette is here somewhere and she needs me. Look," he added as he stepped into the hallway and nothing happened. "There's no magic. You're both jumping at shadows."

The prince strode down the corridor, his shadow growing and shrinking as he walked from the light of one torch to the next. Liam gave Annie a quizzical look and shrugged as he passed her, going after Cozwald.

The whisper grew louder as Annie followed the two young men. The fur was thicker the farther down the hallway they went. Clumps of it cluttered the floor as if someone had brushed a big black dog and dropped the fur on the floor to clean up later, except no one seemed to clean much of anything in this castle.

"This stuff is everywhere," said Cozwald, stopping to shake the fur off his boot. "Keep your eyes open. There must be a big dog here."

Liam bent down to pick up a small clump. "Or a bear," he said, rubbing the fur between his fingers.

The shriek was closer this time, the sound so loud that it made Annie jump and everyone turn their heads to listen. She was still looking the other way when she bumped into Liam. "Why did you stop?" she asked, backing away, and noticed for the first time that the black fur seemed drawn to Liam's and Cozwald's feet, clustering around them like bees drawn to flowers. There was so much fur around them that they had to struggle to pull their feet free. The same fur seemed to avoid Annie entirely.

"It's the fur," she said. "The magic is connected to the fur."

Cozwald laughed. "We didn't need you to tell us that."

Fur flew from the far ends of the hallway, piling up around Liam and the prince. "I can't ... get rid of it!" said Cozwald, his face turning red as he tried to pull his foot free.

"Let me help," said Annie.

The fur moved aside at her approach, leaving a clear path in front of her. She touched Liam first and the fur fell away. After escorting him to a bench, she went back for Cozwald, who was engulfed up to his thighs in what looked like furry boots. The black covering rippled when Annie touched the prince, then slid off as if he'd been greased. The fur undulated behind her as she walked him to the bench, keeping her hand on his arm until he had stepped onto it.

With Annie in the way, the fur was unable to reach its quarry. Loose strands retreated down the hallway, moving together into a large, seething mass. As clumps of fur piled one on top of another, they took on a roughly man-like shape with long fuzzy fingers and toes. When it was almost as tall as Liam, the figure turned its hollow eyes and gaping mouth toward them.

"It's hideous!" exclaimed Cozwald.

"It looks like my great-uncle Elgin!" Liam announced. "My mother always said he was the hairiest man she'd ever met."

"Then I pity your family," said Cozwald.

The beast roared and dragged one foot toward them. Cozwald tightened his grip on his sword. "What does it want?" he asked, and reached up with his free hand to tuck a lock of hair behind his ear.

"I doubt it wants your hair," said Annie. "Look out!"

The fur beast had swiped at Cozwald with its massive hand. When the prince stepped back, he nearly fell off the bench.

"A good offense is the best defense!" shouted Liam. Raising his sword, he jumped to the floor and lunged for the man made of fur.

Cozwald followed Liam and together they hacked at the beast, cutting wedges of fur from its body that crawled back and reattached themselves. The beast seemed to be waiting for something as it stood there, letting the young men stab and cut away pieces without even trying to avoid their blows.

Liam seemed to realize this first, because he stepped aside long enough to study the beast. "That isn't working," he told Cozwald, who continued to rain blows on the giant wad of fur.

"What did you say?" asked the prince, pausing to glance at Liam.

The fur beast lunged, wrapping its frizzy hands around Cozwald's throat.

"Mph!" said the prince, his eyes frantic as he tried to hack at the beast with the side of his blade.

"Oh, for goodness' sake!" said Annie. "Put that thing down before you hurt someone." When the prince continued to wave his sword around, Annie whispered something in Liam's ear. He nodded and jumped forward to knock the sword from Cozwald's hand. The prince's eyes were beginning to bulge when Annie walked up behind the beast and wrapped her arms around its middle. It made a high-pitched keening sound and collapsed in a shower of fur.

Annie coughed and wiped her face. "That's disgusting! I got some in my mouth. Pleh!" She spat, trying to get rid of it.

"You're covered with fur," said Liam, patting her back and arms. "Come help us, Cozwald."

The prince backed away. "And get that fur on me? I'm about to rescue my ladylove. I don't want her to see me looking like I slept in a kennel."

"But it's all right for me to look like this?" asked Annie.

Cozwald shrugged. "That was your choice."

"Be polite to the princess!" Liam growled at the prince. "We're helping you because we chose to, but we can always choose to turn and walk away."

161

Cozwald's eyes flashed and he opened his mouth as if to protest, but he must have seen something in Liam's eyes, because his own gaze dropped and he muttered, "Sorry."

Annie clenched her teeth so she wouldn't say what she had in mind. Before she could unclench them, a groan drew Cozwald to the end of the hallway. Another loud shriek and the sound of crazed laughter made Liam run through a dwindling cloud of drifting black fur to join the prince. "Here, take the other side," Liam told him, indicating one of the benches. Using the bench as a battering ram, they bashed in the door and tore into the room.

Cozwald stumbled over a small trunk that had been left just inside the door. He fell sprawling at the dainty feet of the princess, who looked up from her hand of cards and cried out, her green eyes dark with alarm. The ogre seated on the other side of the table looked equally surprised to see the intruders.

Annie was right behind Liam and Cozwald, certain that she should have gone in first, but when she saw what was inside, she wasn't sure what to think. The room was large and elegantly furnished with a polished stone fireplace and thick rugs in crimson, yellow, and green. A wide bed piled high with warm furs filled one end of the room; the table and chairs occupied the other. The oddly matched couple had been playing cards, and it was obvious that the princess had been winning; a stack of gold coins rested by her elbow, while only a few copper coins littered the ogre's side of the table. The princess was a beautiful young woman with hair as black as night, but she didn't look beautiful with her mouth hanging open as she stared at the intruders, the cards in her hand forgotten. On the other side of the table, a wide grin disappeared from the face of the scraggly bearded ogre, whose eyebrows met in the middle over his bleary red eyes. Seated, he didn't seem to be much taller than the princess, but Annie could see his long legs stretched out under the table.

"Lizette!" shouted Prince Cozwald, scrambling off the floor. "I've come to rescue you, my love!" Grabbing the princess by the arm, he yanked her from the chair and shoved her behind him as he turned to face the ogre.

The ogre's forehead crinkled into a ferocious scowl. "Get your paws off her!" he roared. Shoving the table aside, he sent it crashing to the floor as he heaved himself to his feet. Standing, the ogre was well over seven feet tall and towered over everyone in the room.

"Prepare to die, you foul fiend!" shouted Cozwald, lunging at the ogre with his sword.

The ogre grunted as he tugged a cudgel from the back of his sagging pants. Wielding the nail-studded weapon, he took a step forward and knocked the prince's sword aside with a *clang*. The sword flew out of Cozwald's hand and across the room, leaving the prince defenseless. He looked desperate until he remembered the ax still tucked in the loop on his belt. Flipping his long hair out of his eyes, he stuck out his chin and shouted, "Now you will die, you horrible monster! This is a magic ax made to kill creatures like you!"

Torchlight reflected off the etching on the metal head of the ax, sparkling in a way that might have convinced Annie that it was magical if she hadn't known better. The ogre saw the ax at the same time and took a step back as if he, too, thought that it was magic. When Lizette sobbed and threw up her hand in appeal, the ogre glanced at her, then back at Cozwald, and he growled. Raising his cudgel high, he swiped it at the prince, who swung his ax at the same time. One of the weapons would have connected if Lizette hadn't stuck her foot out and tripped Cozwald. The prince went down and the cudgel whistled past his head.

Liam jumped into the fray now, beating the ogre back with powerful blows of his sword. It was obvious that Liam was a much better swordsman than Cozwald, who scooted out of the way as the ogre used his cudgel to ward off Liam's blows. Annie was so wrapped up in watching them that she almost didn't notice Lizette take a candlestick from a niche in the wall and sneak up behind Liam.

"No!" Annie shouted as the princess raised the candlestick over Liam's head.

Annie wasn't the only one who had seen Lizette, however, because Cozwald threw his arms around her and

164

dragged her away from the fight. "What are you doing, Lizette?" he asked as she struggled to get free. "We've come to rescue you!"

"What makes you think I need to be rescued?" she asked, and stomped on his toes. Cozwald yelped and let go of the princess, who turned and brandished the candlestick in his face.

Cozwald backed away, fending her off with his hand. "Your father said an ogre had kidnapped you, yet I find you playing cards with the monster. Do you mean to say that you like it here?"

"He isn't a monster!" said Lizette. "And I'd rather be with him than with anyone else in the world. I'm happier with Grimsby than I've been in my entire life."

"But he's an ogre!"

"Yes, and you have a head shaped like a cantaloupe, but I don't hold that against you."

"I do?" Cozwald said, reaching up to feel his skull.

"Grimsby is special. He makes me laugh."

Cozwald blinked. "I know they say that no one has ever heard you laugh, but that was you laughing earlier, wasn't it?"

"Liam," Annie called. "I think you should hear this."

The ogre, who had been busy fighting off Liam's blade, seemed relieved when the young man stepped back.

"If you'd grown up the way I did, you wouldn't laugh, either," said Lizette. "My mother died when I was born. My nursemaid told me that my parents laughed all the

165

time, but after my mother died my father never smiled again. When I was little, he scolded me whenever I laughed. He said that my mother died because of me and I didn't have any right to be happy. I grew up thinking that laughter was bad. None of my suitors made me laugh, including you, and I thought I was going to be miserable for the rest of my life until I met Grimsby."

"Where did you meet him?" asked Liam, eyeing the ogre.

"I was out riding with my ladies-in-waiting one day and we ran into Grimsby. He'd gotten pine tar on his hands and picked up a goose, which stuck to him no matter what he did. It was the funniest thing I'd ever seen and I laughed until my sides hurt. My ladies ran away screaming, but Grimsby and I became friends. When I couldn't stand living at home any longer, the only place I wanted to go was Grimsby's castle."

"Does your father know this?"

"He should. Grimsby and I are engaged and I've already sent Father an invitation to the wedding. I doubt he'll come, though. He's probably embarrassed that I ran away from home to come here. I've been living in this castle for three weeks now and I've never been happier."

Cozwald looked disappointed when he asked, "So you don't need rescuing?"

"No, but thank you anyway," Lizette said.

"Then I guess our work here is done," said Cozwald. Bending his knee in a courtly bow, he added, "I wish you both well," then turned to Liam and Annie. "Come, my friends, it's time we go. We've disrupted their lives enough already."

Annie glanced back as they were leaving the room and saw that Lizette and the ogre were holding hands. She also saw the way they were looking at each other. It was a warm, tender look and one she'd never seen before, not even on the faces of her parents, who everyone said were madly in love. *It's the look of true love,* she thought. *If a princess and an ogre can find it, why can't I?*

Once he'd left Lizette, all Cozwald seemed to want was to get out of the ogre's castle as quickly as possible. "That's the last time I help a damsel in distress," he muttered as they hurried down the stairs to the room with the dirty table.

"At least she's happy now," said Annie.

"Huh!" said Cozwald. "She's marrying an ogre! I bet their marriage doesn't last a month."

Annie glanced at the prince, noting the sour look on his face. "I'm sure you're right," she said. "She was too happy. When she gets tired of being happy, she'll run back to her father for a good dose of miserableness."

CHAPTER 12

AFTER SPENDING AN uncomfortable night in the forest, Annie and Liam went with Cozwald to see his cousin. Because the cousin was a prince, Annie had expected to go to a castle, or at least a large, imposing manor house, and was surprised when they rode through the forest to the edge of a mist-shrouded swamp.

"He should be somewhere around here," said Cozwald as he dismounted from his horse. "Emilio!" he called. "It's me, Cozwald!"

"Is his castle in this swamp?" asked Annie as they waited for the prince to appear.

Cozwald laughed. "He hasn't lived in a castle in years. Emilio comes here to reminisce about some things and forget about others. Ah, there he is now. Emilio, I'd like you to meet some friends of mine."

At first Annie couldn't see anything, but then a shape moving in the swirling mist resolved into a handsome yet bedraggled young man. His hair was darker than his cousin's—almost the color of walnuts, and his features were more refined than Cozwald's, but she could see a family resemblance. The biggest difference between them, however, was their eyes. While Cozwald's eyes smiled when he did, Emilio's eyes looked as if he had known nothing but sadness.

"Princess Annabelle, I'd like you to meet my cousin Prince Emilio," said Cozwald. "His mother is my father's sister. He's also my second cousin on my mother's side. Emilio, the princess and her escort are looking for someone to kiss her sister, and you'll never guess who that is! If you go with her, you stand a chance of marrying Princess Gwendolyn, the most beautiful princess in all the kingdoms!"

Prince Emilio gave Annie a halfhearted smile, then turned back to his cousin. "What's wrong with Gwendolyn?" he asked. "If she wants to marry me, there must be something wrong with her. No one in her right mind would want to marry me." His Adam's apple bobbed when he swallowed and he blinked at the same time.

"Gwendolyn is asleep," said Liam. "And will stay that way until her true love kisses her."

Emilio looked puzzled. "Why would you think I'm her true love? Once you get to know me, I'm sure you'd see that I'm not at all suitable."

"We don't know who her true love is, so we're inviting all the unattached princes we meet to kiss her.

We're hoping that one of you will be the right one," said Liam.

"That doesn't sound very good," Annie said.

"Maybe," Liam said, shrugging, "but it's the truth, isn't it?"

"What about you?" Emilio asked his cousin Cozwald. "Are you going to kiss her, too?"

Cozwald looked surprised. "I hadn't thought about it. I mean, I was planning to marry Lizette, but that didn't work out. I suppose I could kiss Gwendolyn. It would certainly make my parents happy. They've been after me to get married for years."

"Then there's no need for me to go," Emilio said, looking doleful. He glanced at Annie, saying, "You wouldn't want me to kiss your sister if you knew more about me."

"Emilio is a little self-conscious about his past," said Cozwald. "He was married to a lovely princess who bore him two sweet children. They were living happily ever after until one day he rode past the swamp and his horse's hooves splashed mud on a nasty fairy. The fairy was furious and turned him into a frog."

"I lived in the swamp for season after season until a princess came looking for frogs," said Emilio. "Apparently there was a shortage of available princes and she'd heard that kissing a frog was a good way to find one. She kissed me and was delighted when I turned into my old self, but when she learned that I was already married she dumped me for the next handsome frog to come along."

"You mean handsome prince," prompted Cozwald. A fly landed on Annie's wrist, tickling her. She shook her hand to dislodge the fly and it flew off, buzzing. Emilio watched the fly go, his eyes tracking it as it zigzagged back into the swamp. Cozwald nudged his cousin with his elbow.

"That's right," Emilio hurried to say. "So I rushed home to see my family, only to learn that my stepmother had given my wife a poisoned apple and sold my children to a woodcutter who took them with him when he moved away. I've scoured the kingdom looking for them, but no one has seen them anywhere."

"Emilio was a wreck," Cozwald said. "My mother invited him to stay with us, but he was so depressed that he made everyone else depressed. After a few weeks, my father made him go home. He spends most of his time in the swamp now."

"It's the only place that doesn't remind me of my family," said Emilio, dabbing at unshed tears glistening in his eyes. "Even so, my memories torment me every minute of the day. My wife was as pretty as a swamp rose and even sweeter. Little Clara was only a baby when I was turned into a frog, but Tomas was a strapping lad who could already ride a horse and draw a bow. If I could have anything in the world, it would be to have my family with me again. Without them, life just hasn't been worth living."

Annie felt sorry for the poor man, but she could see

how he could make everyone depressed. She wondered if they'd been a little hasty in making the offer to Emilio.

A tree branch cracked in the forest behind them. Emilio jumped into the air, landing three feet away. Muck geysered out from under his feet, splashing Annie with droplets from head to toe. He looked wildly around for a moment, then seemed to remember himself and came back to stand beside his cousin, looking even more downhearted. "Sorry about that," he said. "I can't seem to help myself."

"Uh-huh," said Annie. Not only was he depressing to be near, but it looked as though he hadn't lost his froggie ways yet; she wasn't sure she wanted him as her brother-in-law. Even so, that didn't mean she wouldn't help him if she could. "I might have met your children," she said, trying to brush off some of the bigger clumps of muck. "At least, I met a boy named Tomas and his little sister, Clara. We were in a wicked witch's cottage, but they ran away when we escaped. They said something about living with a woodcutter who wasn't really their father."

Emilio's eyes lit up and suddenly he seemed younger and more alive. "That must be them! Where did you see them? Is it far from here?"

"The cottage was in the forest south of the royal castle of Treecrest by, oh, I'd say, twelve to fifteen miles. I met a bear who was an enchanted prince and asked him to keep an eye out for them. His name was Beldegard. He was very nice and I'm sure he would have kept the children safe, if he found them."

Cozwald looked thoughtful as he rubbed his chin. "I used to know a Prince Beldegard. He was my aunt's sister's husband's second cousin. A nice fellow, as I recall."

"I have to go!" said Emilio. "My little ones need me! I'll look for them until I find them, even if it takes me season after season. Thank you for telling me," he said, taking Annie's hand in his and giving it a hard squeeze. "I haven't been this happy since before Voracia turned me into a frog. Now, if you'll excuse me, I must get ready and—"

"Did you say Voracia?" asked Annie. "That's who I'm looking for! She's the one who cast the spell on my sister."

"Then perhaps I can help you just as you helped me," said Emilio. "Voracia lives only a few miles from here in the Great Greasy Swamp. I'd take you there myself, but I want to go find my children. Perhaps you can show them the way, Cozwald?"

"I think I should go with you," said his cousin. "You may need my help."

"Just give us directions," said Annie. "I'm sure Liam and I can find it."

After saying their farewells to Cozwald and his cousin, Annie and Liam rode around the edge of the swamp, looking for the way in that the princes had described. They were still looking a few hours later, crossing and recrossing the same general area, when they paused by a patch of ground choked with swamp briars.

"I think we should go back and start again," said Liam.

"Just a moment," said Annie. "I thought I heard something." Dismounting from her horse's back, she stepped carefully across the sodden ground and stopped to listen near a clump of bushes with longer prickers than the rest. A discordant series of notes drew her close enough to know that magic surrounded the bushes. "The path is this way," she said, and kicked the closest plant. The entire clump broke free and rolled aside at her touch.

Liam tried to nudge his horse closer, but the animal tossed its head and refused to move. When he dug his heels into its side, the usually calm horse danced backward and fought the reins.

"It looks like we'll have to walk from here," said Liam.

Once again they tied their horses to a tree and started out on foot. The path twisted and turned, crossing over hillocks and narrow strips of land that wound between murky, weed-choked water and deep, scum-frothed pools. Some sections of the path were made of grass, some of stone, and some of crushed insect casings that glistened in the sunlight.

The sky became overcast as they moved deeper into the swamp. After a time the clouds seemed to settle around them as a thick fog smelling of dead things and rot moved in. The fog plagued Liam, swirling around him so that he couldn't see the ground and had difficulty staying on the path. Annie didn't have any problem, however;

the fog thinned to pale wisps at her approach and crowded in behind her once she'd passed by. She might not have noticed when Liam missed his footing and sank knee deep in the muck if he hadn't cried out in surprise.

"Need a hand?" Annie asked, reaching to help him.

"No thanks," said Liam as he struggled to pull himself out of the muck. "I already have two. I would like to have my feet back, however." Spying a low-hanging branch, he grabbed hold and tried to pull himself free, but it held for only a moment before breaking with a loud *crack!* Liam sat down hard in the mud. "I think the swamp is working against me."

"Let me help," said Annie, grabbing the back of his tunic.

Suddenly the mud that had held him like frozen molasses let go. Annie tugged and he slid back, nearly knocking her over when his shoulder hit her knees. She kept her hand on his sleeve as he clambered onto solid ground, but let go when he stepped away from her to stomp the mud from his feet. A vine immediately wrapped itself around his ankle and began to pull him off the path.

"I think you should hold my hand," Annie said, extending hers toward him.

"That won't be necessary—," Liam began, but Annie grabbed hold anyway. The vine shuddered and let go. "Oh," he said. "I guess it will."

Liam's hand was nearly twice as big as hers, the skin

rough and the sides of his fingers calloused from long hours of practice with bow and arrows. She liked the way it enveloped her hand.

"Some of my non-magic transfers to you when we touch," said Annie.

Liam nodded. "Like when you pulled me off the kelpie's back. I should have remembered that sooner."

The look he gave her was warmer than that of a normal guard, or even a normal friend. His eyes lingered on her face, and she could feel heat rising up her neck to color her cheeks.

"Don't let go," he said, giving her hand a squeeze.

"I won't," said Annie, and she had to force herself to look away.

They had walked a good distance into the swamp and Annie was beginning to wonder if they had gone the wrong way after all when the path ended abruptly. Suddenly, the tall grass surrounding them began to wave furiously and two small figures the size of human infants jumped out, landing only feet away.

"What are you doing here?" asked the taller of the two. His sharp-featured face looked out from beneath a mass of feathery white hair, looking to Annie like a grumpy hedgehog in a patch of dandelions that had gone to seed. The black tunic and leggings that he wore were made from strips of sewn snakeskin that quivered when he moved.

The other sprite seemed shy, and stayed behind his

friend to peek around his shoulder. His coppery red hair was the same color as his clothes, and his pale face looked ghostly white. His tunic, created from autumn leaves, made a crinkling sound when he brushed against the other sprite, shedding dried, leafy fragments.

"We're here to see the fairy Voracia," said Annie.

"Liar!" said the taller sprite. "No one comes to see Voracia. They come here because they're lost or because someone has dragged them, kicking and yelling."

The other sprite tweaked his friend's pointed ear. "They might be ensorcelled, Poke 'Em. Or maybe they're evil witches done up to look like no-account humans."

"We'd better take them to Voracia. She'll know what to do with trespassers."

"Maybe she'll turn them into slime mold like that man who wandered into the swamp last week."

"I hope not," said Poke 'Em. "I stepped in him the other day and he oozed onto my favorite shoes. I don't think I'll ever get the stain out. Come along, you two," he told the humans, wiggling a stick in their direction. "Voracia will want to see you right away."

The two sprites ushered Annie and Liam through the swamp, one sprite pinching them when they took too long crossing the squishy ground, while the other poked them with his stick when they lost their footing. Gray fog drifted across their path, evaporating at the sprites' approach. Now and then Annie caught a glimpse of a large white outcropping in the distance. The fog hid it for a while, then there it was again, closer and even big-ger, leering at them like an enormous skull carved out of stone.

They entered a part of the swamp where limbless, blackened tree trunks stood sentinel. A small flock of crows circled overhead, watching humans and sprites. Poke 'Em shouted at the crows, but it was his smaller friend who found pebbles and chucked them at the birds.

Once more the fog closed in, and even though it didn't come near Annie and Liam, it kept them from see-ing more than a few feet away. When the view cleared again, they were standing on a patch of dead swamp-grass twenty yards from what Annie now saw wasn't stone at all, but the giant skull of the world's largest bird, the roc.

The skull was located on an island not much wider than the skull itself. Annie eyed it with interest as she and Liam followed Poke 'Em. They were nearing the island when Liam bent down and whispered in Annie's ear, "I've never seen a roc's skull before. Where do you suppose the rest of it is?"

Poke 'Em waved his stick in their direction, gesturing for them to be quiet. Annie noticed that the little sprite held back and let his friend approach the island. The smaller sprite hadn't seemed so mean the last few hun-dred yards, not since the last time he'd pinched Annie, and he'd begun to look less surly and more fearful. Poke

'Em was looking a little less nasty, too, even though he hadn't touched her. Unlike his friend, he didn't look the least bit afraid. He was about to say something when they heard muted voices coming from the skull.

"... the wickedest one in the land," said a harsh voice.

"Well, you, but not by much," responded a voice so faint that Annie had to strain to hear it. "There's a new witch in the neighborhood whom everyone's talking about."

"What are they saying about her?" growled the harsher voice.

"Her name is Terobella and she's almost as terrible as you. I heard that she eats baby bunnies and downy chicks for breakfast."

"Sounds yummy," said the voice that must have been Voracia's. "Maybe I'll have to invite myself over for breakfast. Where does she live?"

"In the deep dark swamp where the little snakelets dwell, where globs of scum float past your toes and give off a pungent smell."

"You mean she's my next-door neighbor?"

"That's what I heard."

"I'll have to look into this."

Annie could hear the grating sound of the fairy's magic, but there was another sound as well. A faint melody repeated itself over and over and grew louder each time the whispery voice spoke, making Annie think it was the roc skull itself.

"By the way," said the roc. "Pinch 'Em and Poke 'Em have brought two humans to see you."

"Really?" said Voracia, and her face appeared in one of the roc's eye holes. "Well, well, what have we here?"

"I just told you, Pinch 'Em, Poke 'Em, and two humans," the skull replied.

"I know that, dummy! But who are they and what do they want?"

"Hmph!" said the skull. "I can't answer that if I'm such a dummy. You're just going to have to find out for yourself."

Voracia scowled and thumped the edge of the eye socket with her fist, but when the roc skull remained silent, the fairy turned her glare on Annie and Liam. She was a tall woman with sharp, angular features and dark, sunken eyes. Her gown was black with the skulls of newborn baby mice dangling like beads from a chain around her neck. A copper and brown striped snakeskin wound through her silver hair, lending her outfit its only touch of color.

The fairy tapped her long, thin fingers against the bone of the skull's eye socket. "Well, out with it! Who are you and why are you here?"

Poke 'Em prodded Annie and Liam with his stick, making them walk through a gap in the side of the skull. The air inside was cold and damp, and a draft rose from a set of steps that descended from just inside the back of the skull to deep into the ground. "Pinch 'Em and I found them wandering through the swamp," said the sprite. "They said they wanted to talk to you."

"They *must* be crazy," said the skull.

"Toss them into the bottomless pool," Voracia declared. "Normal humans are bad enough. I don't need crazy ones lost in my swamp."

"But we're not crazy!" Annie hurried to say. "We weren't lost, either. We came to the swamp because we need your help. You cast a spell on my sister sixteen years ago and we need you to tell us how to undo it."

"How refreshing," murmured the skull. "She's using the direct approach. That hasn't worked on Voracia in years."

The fairy laughed. It was a jarring sound, like a sharp-toothed rasp scraping on metal, or an iron bar ramming home into the lock of a dungeon door. "Why would you think that I would want to help you?" the fairy asked.

"Because of what will happen if you don't," Annie said, and reached out to grab hold of the fairy's wrist. Even in the few seconds that their skin made contact, Annie could hear the sound of Voracia's magic growing fainter.

Voracia tried to pull away, but Annie tightened her grip until her fingers dug into the fairy's flesh. "You'll help me," Annie told her, "because if you don't, I won't be able to help my family, so there won't be any reason for me to go home. I might as well stay here with you then."

"Uh, Voracia," said the skull, its voice fading.

"Something's happening to me." The sound of its magic stopped as the skull became silent.

"Let go of me, you disgusting creature! How dare you touch me!" The fairy's dark eyes snapping with fury, she thrust Annie away, whipped out her magic wand, and pointed it at the girl. "To the bottomless pool!" she screamed. A flash of orange light shot from the wand, hit Annie, and bounced back at the fairy, who vanished in an instant.

Annie hadn't had time to cover her ears, so the sound of the rebounding magic hit her like a clap of thunder. She staggered back, falling into Liam's arms.

"Where did she go?" Poke 'Em asked even as he backed away.

Liam's lips brushed Annie's ear when he bent down and said, "Are you all right?"

"I'm fine," she replied. She let him help her to her feet.

Suddenly Voracia returned, dripping wet and furious. She staggered, bumped into Annie, and they both fell down in a heap on top of Liam. Annie set her hand on the fairy's shoulder, trying to push her away. Voracia rolled off the two humans and hopped to her feet. The sound of her magic had dwindled even more in the brief time she'd been touching Annie, and her clothes looked older and more ragged than a dip in the water could make them.

Voracia tossed her head, flinging her hair behind her and showering Annie and Liam with droplets of muddy water. "How did you reverse my magic?" the fairy asked through clenched teeth. A freshwater snail oozed off her chin and plopped onto the floor, landing in the puddle of water that was forming around her shoes.

"I didn't do anything," Annie declared. "You did it to yourself."

"Don't be absurd," the fairy said, raising her wand again. This time the orange light was pale and lasted for only a second, just long enough to make a soft fizzing sound.

Annie glanced behind her at the sound of splashing feet. Poke 'Em and Pinch 'Em were running away, jumping from hillock to patch of soggy ground even as a light breeze carried off the last wisps of fog.

"What kind of powerful magic do you have that you can do this to me?" wailed Voracia, her chin trembling. A dimple had appeared in her cheek and her features no longer looked so sharp.

"My only magic is that magic doesn't work around me," said Annie. "If you touch me, your magic will fade. If you're even near me, your magic will fade, too."

"And if you try to cast a spell at her, it will bounce back onto you," said Liam.

"That's the most horrible thing I've ever heard!" cried

Voracia. "Whatever turned you into such an unspeakable monster?"

"My fairy godmother's magic," said Annie, smiling.

A crow cawed, and Annie turned her head. A small flock was circling the island, peering through the holes in the skull.

"Those chatterboxes are going to tell everyone what has happened to me!" howled Voracia. "That witch Terobella is going to be the wickedest in the land and I'll be the laughingstock of the swamp."

"Not if you help me," said Annie. "Tell me what I need to know. We'll leave and your magic will get strong again. Sixteen years ago you cast a spell on my sister, Gwendolyn, that would make her die when she pricked her finger on the spindle of a spinning wheel. Another fairy at my sister's christening changed the curse so that instead of dying, Gwendolyn would fall asleep for a hundred years only to awaken at her true love's kiss. I've found princes to kiss her, but now I need you to do whatever it takes so that we don't have to wait for one hundred years. You cast the original curse, so it's up to you to undo it."

"I'd forgotten all about that curse. Haven't thought about it for years. I can't take it back, if that's what you want," said Voracia. "However, I can give you something that will make the time shorter."

"I want it to end now!" said Annie.

"That's what I said!" Voracia grumbled. "Stay here, I'll be right back." She headed for the stairs.

"I think we'll go with you," said Liam, setting his hand on the hilt of his sword. "I don't trust her if we can't see her," he whispered to Annie.

"I don't trust her even if I can see her," Annie replied.

The stairwell was damp and dark, but the passage underneath was worse. Water flowed over their feet as they followed Voracia deep underground. The smell of bat dung met them as the passage curved, but the fairy turned into a cave lined with trunks and boxes before they encountered any bats.

Choosing one of the trunks, Voracia reached inside and pulled out a large, dusty bottle. "Here, give your sister a sip of this when she wakes and you can forget the hundred years part."

"If I give this to her and anything goes wrong, you know I'll be back," said Annie as she reached for the bottle. "I'll move in and you'll never be rid of me."

"Never mind!" said Voracia, snatching the bottle away. After putting it back, she rummaged in another trunk for a moment, finally pulling out another bottle just as old and dusty. "Here, give her some of this instead, but make sure she drinks it within three minutes of waking or she'll fall asleep again and nothing will wake her in less than a hundred years. Now go away and don't ever come back."

Annie took the bottle and handed it to Liam. "We won't, provided this works and that you never bother my family again."

"I wouldn't go near them for all the poisoned apples in the world," said Voracia. "Not if it means I would have to see you!"

CHAPTER 13

ANNIE WAS RELIEVED when they finally left the swamp behind, but Liam refused to relax. "Something's not right," he said as they settled into their saddles. "We're being watched. I can feel it."

"Do you think Voracia..."

Liam shook his head. "I don't think it's Voracia, or anything magical. I think it's... Wait! Look over there!"

"I don't see anything."

"I don't either now, but I could have sworn I saw someone peeking at us from behind those trees."

"Maybe it was a wood nymph or a fairy," Annie suggested.

"Maybe," said Liam, although he didn't sound convinced. "You stay here while I go look around and—"

A twig cracked behind them, startling them both. "Let's get out of here," said Annie. "This swamp is creepy and it will be dark in a few hours. I don't want to be any-where near Voracia when the sun goes down."

"There's an inn only an hour's ride from here," Liam said. "It's not very fancy, but the bedding is clean and the food is good."

"I couldn't ask for anything more," said Annie.

She tried to carry on a conversation with Liam as they rode through the forest, but he was paying more atten-tion to what was going on around them than to what she had to say. Although he kept turning his head to the side as if he heard riders in the woods, Annie neither saw nor heard anything unusual. The road soon took them out of the forest and across farmland where low stone walls divided the fields that covered the rolling hills. Every time they reached the top of a hill, Liam stopped to look back. Annie turned as well, but the way was always clear.

They reached the crossroads where the inn was located without seeing anyone. While the hostler led the horses into the stable, Liam went in search of the innkeeper to arrange for rooms and a bath for the princess. Hearing a crowd in the taproom, Annie peeked through the doorway. Travelers sitting down to an early supper already occupied most of the tables. She smiled at the first curious glances, but when she saw the way people were looking at her swamp-stained clothes and disheveled hair, she stepped outside to wait for Liam.

Two men stood by the entrance to the stables watch-ing the inn. When one of them noticed Annie, he spoke to the other and they both started toward her. Although they were dressed in rough homespun, they looked vaguely familiar.

Annie was still trying to decide where she might have seen them when a third man came out of the inn behind her. "Princess Annabelle?" he said.

"Yes?" replied Annie, turning to face him. In an instant, one of the men approaching from the stable threw a cloth bag over her head while the other grabbed her hands and tried to tie them behind her back. She kicked out at the men and opened her mouth to scream just as the third man knocked her on the head with something hard. With a soft moan, Annie collapsed in a heap at their feet.

~

When Annie woke, her head was pounding and her mouth tasted like sweaty feet. She sat up and groaned as the throbbing in her head worsened. A light flickered overhead. Annie stared at it for some time before it registered in her mind that it was a guttering torch about to go out. Darkness was creeping closer when she stood and staggered against a wall, her head reeling. It occurred to her that she was in a dungeon and she wondered vaguely how she might have gotten there. Then it all came back—the swamp, Liam's suspicion that they were being followed, and the men at the inn. She remembered now where she had seen the men before.

It was in the woods shortly after she left the secret tunnel leading from her parents' castle. The men had been talking about her even then.

The torch was getting fainter when Annie took a step and nearly tripped over a basket. Glancing down, she saw that it was filled with new torches, waiting to be lit. Snatching up one of the torches, she held it to the dying light and held her breath until a flame blossomed. Thinking that if her kidnappers had provided her with light, they might have left something else, Annie raised her head to look around.

She was in a circular room with a low ceiling and a set of stairs at the opposite side. The stones of the wall beside her were lighter than the rest and the mortar was still damp, as if someone had recently filled in a hole. Water burbled in a stone basin only a few yards away. Apparently the tower had been built over a spring, providing fresh water for whoever was unfortunate enough to be trapped inside. Barrels and trunks were scattered across the floor, some stacked, others open and partially emptied. Piles of clothes and shoes were strewn across the floor, forcing Annie to pick her way with care as she headed to the stairs.

The stairs had been built against the wall and were open on the side facing into the room. When Annie reached the first step, she paused and raised the torch high. Although the stairs were dark beyond the reach of the light, there was no door to block her way. It was obvious that she was in a tower, but as she climbed, she wondered just how high it might be. Passing the floor of the next level, she looked around long enough to see that it was empty, and continued up the stairs. The third and fourth levels were empty as well. The stairs ended at the fifth level in a room with a high ceiling and open windows framing the night sky.

As Annie stepped into the room, a large shape rose up, startling her until she heard it hoot. "Shoo!" Annie shouted, waving the torch at the owl. The bird swerved and flew through one of the windows, blocking her view of the twinkling stars for a moment.

Crinkling her nose at the pungent odor of owl, Annie began to explore the room. It was a bedchamber with a bed against one wall and a table and chair against another. With an ornate headboard carved with hummingbirds and flowers, the bed would have been pretty if its rumpled covers hadn't been so mussed, as if the sleeper had just gotten up. Gowns, tunics, and undergarments were strewn across the floor. Annie found a scarf draped across the foot of the bed. It was the kind that could be worn in a lady's hair, much like the kind Annie had worn on occasion. This one was dirty, however, and smelled of perfume. Annie picked up a gown by one sleeve. It smelled of unwashed body as well as perfume, and showed stains from food and drink.

"A woman lived here," Annie murmured to herself. "She must have just left."

Hoping to find some hint as to who it might have been, she made a quick inspection of the room. The wind was picking up, however, and she began to shiver as the temperature dropped. Annie dragged a blanket from the bed and made herself a cozy nest on the floor, letting the bed block most of the wind. Dousing the torch wasn't easy, but she'd found a flint on the table and knew she could relight the torch when she needed it again.

As the wind whistled through the tower, Annie huddled on the floor and pulled the blanket close. Eventually, her eyes drifted shut; she never noticed when the wind died down and the owl swooped past the window.

Sunlight was streaming through the windows on the east side of the tower when Annie woke the next morning. She was yawning widely when she saw that there were shutters on either side of each window, something she would have found useful the night before if only she had noticed them. Closing her mouth, she felt a hair on her tongue. She wiped her face to brush the hair aside, but nothing happened. Although her hands were dirty, she stuck her finger and thumb in her mouth, and pulled out the hair ... and pulled and pulled. The hair wasn't all the way in her mouth, just running through it. She finally got it out and examined it with disgust. The hair was blond and so long that she had to stand to measure it against her own height. Annie was about five feet tall, and the hair was nearly ten times longer. The thought that anyone could have hair that long turned her stomach, especially when she thought about it being in her mouth.

Annie walked to the window, thinking she might see a castle or village or at least people she could call to, but there was nothing to see except trees. After checking the view from another window, she made a circuit of the room; the trees seemed to go on forever. She was leaning against the sill of the last window when she noticed a clump of long blond hair snagged on the ledge. Backing away from the sill, she noticed another hair on the floor. When she bent down, she discovered that they were all over the floor...and the bed and the chair and in all the clothes. Grimacing, she was trying to decide what to do with all the hair when she heard a voice calling from outside the tower.

"Rapunzel, Rapunzel, let down your hair!"

Thank goodness! Someone who can help me get out of here! Annie thought, and ran across the room to the window where she'd found the clump of hair. A young man stood at the base of the tower, his horse already tied to the nearest tree. He was squinting and shading his eyes when he looked up, so Annie wasn't sure he could really see her.

"I'm sorry, but there's no one here by that name," called Annie. "Would you mind helping me down though? I seem to be trapped up here, and I need to get out. I have to get back to my kingdom."

"I don't understand," the young man began. "I'm Prince Mortimer and I've come to visit my beloved, Rapunzel. Are you sure she isn't there?"

Annie shook her head. "I've looked everywhere. There's no one here but me."

The prince muttered to himself before looking up at Annie again. "Say, if she isn't there, why don't you let down *your* hair so I can climb up?"

"You're joking, right?" Annie's hair reached to the back of her knees, but she never let it get any longer. She thought it was hard enough to deal with as it was. Besides, just as she had resented it when Prince Andreas had seemed to think that she and her sister were interchangeable, she didn't like the way Mortimer seemed to think he could swap Rapunzel for her. It wasn't a topic she wanted to broach with this stranger, however, so instead she said, "My hair isn't nearly long enough to reach you. Tell me, does Rapunzel have long blond hair?"

"She has the most glorious long blond hair and she lets it down every time I come by. I climb up and we enjoy each other's company for the entire day. I look forward to Wednesdays every week."

"I bet you do," Annie said. "Why didn't you ever rescue the poor girl?"

Prince Mortimer looked affronted. "Rapunzel wouldn't let me. She said that a witch had put her there and if I took her out, the witch would come after us and kill us both. She said that she wouldn't mind dying, but

194

she loved me too much for that. So how about it? Will you let down your hair so I can climb up?"

"I told you that I can't. Why don't you help me come down there instead?"

"I don't have a ladder," said the prince.

"It would take an awfully long ladder to reach this window. I don't suppose you know how to climb up?"

"Pardon me?"

Annie sighed. "Never mind. If you see a young man named Liam, please tell him that Princess Annie is in this tower and give him the directions."

"I'll tell him if I happen to run across him," said Prince Mortimer, "but I'm not going to go looking for some stranger."

Annie watched as the young man rode away. After spending one night in the tower, she could imagine how bleak Rapunzel's life must have seemed locked away there for what she thought was forever. *She must really have loved Mortimer to refuse to let him rescue her,* Annie thought. Closing her eyes, she pictured herself in the poor girl's place, but the prince she imagined didn't look anything like Mortimer. Instead it was Liam's face she saw, looking at her the way he had just before he kissed her outside the ogre's castle.

Annie's mood immediately soured. If Liam had shown up at that very minute, she probably would have snapped at him. He wasn't a prince and they couldn't be together, but he'd kissed her nonetheless, and then not said a word about it afterward. She felt like a fool, mooning over a young man who didn't care enough to tell her that he had special feelings for her, if he really did.

She had no doubt that Liam was already looking for her and would find her eventually, although the thought of so much time being wasted when she had none to waste made her anxious. If Liam came soon, all the better, but if he didn't, she would do what she could to rescue herself.

Annie glanced around the tower room. There was nothing here to help her, not even a mirror to reflect light in the hope that someone would see it. Her stomach rumbled, making it harder to ignore the hunger that was eating at her. Although she didn't like the thought of returning to the dark room at the bottom of the tower, it seemed to be the only place she could find food. Using the flint she'd found, she relit the torch and started down the stairs.

The air in the bottom room seemed almost unbearably stuffy and close. Annie looked for food first, and after setting aside bread soft with fuzzy mold and dried meat so hard she knew she risked breaking a tooth if she bit it, she was pleased to find a small, as yet unopened crock of pickled vegetables and half a wheel of moldy cheese. Taking the knife she found stuck in the wheel, she cut off the mold and discarded it before savoring the rich, nutty flavor of the cheese.

She was thirsty now, so she knelt beside the stone basin and took a long, cool sip of water. It tasted surprisingly fresh and when she dropped a few crumbs of cheese in the water, she saw that they swirled away down an overflow hole hidden in the side of the basin. Annie wondered where the water went, so she reached under the lip of the basin and felt for the hole; it was too small for her hand to fit in. When she tried to move the basin in the hope that there might be a larger opening underneath, it was far too heavy.

Carrying the torch in one hand, Annie began to inspect the wall. The stones were all firmly set, however, including those that had been used to fill in the newest opening. She thought about using the cheese knife to dig through the mortar, but it would take too much time.

Discouraged, Annie filled a jug with water and took it along with the crock of pickled vegetables and the remains of the cheese wheel up the stairs to the room at the top. She'd really been hoping that she would find some secret latch or hidden door, but if there was any such thing, the builder had hidden it too well.

Not sure how long she'd be stuck in the tower, Annie decided to make herself comfortable. The room was a mess, and Annie couldn't bear the thought of living in it the way Rapunzel had left it. After nibbling another piece of cheese, she began to clean the room, tossing all the soiled clothes in a pile and stripping the filthy bedding off the bed. Seeing the condition of the bed underneath, she decided that she'd rather sleep on the floor.

Annie was thinking about going back to the first level to look for a broom when she noticed that some strands of Rapunzel's hair were stuck to her clothes. She pulled off a strand that had draped itself across her shoulder and down her back. She intended to drop it out the window, but on the way there she got an idea; the more she thought about it, the more perfect it seemed.

She moved the chair, placing it in a pool of sunlight, and would have moved the table as well, but it was so heavy that she couldn't budge it. After collecting a few dozen strands of hair, she took them with her to the chair. The sun was high in the sky when she began to braid them. When she had braided three-quarters of their length, she knotted more strands to the braid and began to braid them in as well. By the time the sun set, the hair rope was long, yet still not long enough for what she needed.

The night was mild and the sky was clear, so she didn't bother to close the shutters. After a quick meal, she wrapped herself in a blanket and lay down so that she could look out the window at the same stars she saw from her bedroom window at home. The familiar sight made her feel a little less lost and alone.

Even before Annie ate anything the next morning,

she returned to braiding the hair. She worked with a frenzy that made her clumsy at times, so she had to slow down and undo some of the plaiting more than once. Intent on her work, she didn't hear her visitor at first.

"Rapunzel, Rapunzel," he called again. "Let down your hair!"

Annie dropped the braid and jumped to her feet. Whoever this was, perhaps he would help her get out of the tower. She ran to the window and leaned over the ledge to see a young man standing down below with his cap in one hand and a bouquet in the other.

"I'm beginning to get a picture of this girl Rapunzel," Annie muttered to herself. "Rapunzel isn't here," she shouted to the young man. "Tell me, is she a princess from a local kingdom?"

"Is this a trick question?" the young man called back. "My darling Rapunzel isn't a princess. She's the beautiful daughter of two peasants and was brought up by an evil witch in this very tower. Now how about letting down your hair so I can come up and spend the day with my beloved. Tell her that Prince Ludlow has arrived."

"I already told you, she isn't here."

"What do you mean she isn't here? It's Thursday. I'm sure she's expecting me."

"She's gone. I've looked everywhere and I can tell you with absolute certainty that I am the only one here."

Even from a distance, the young man looked disappointed. He held the flowers as if he was about to throw them away, but then he paused and glanced up at Annie again. "I don't suppose that you could let your hair down and—"

"No! My hair isn't long enough. Let me guess, you don't have a ladder."

"Why no, I've never needed one."

Annie sighed. "And you don't have any other way to get up or down, do you?"

The young man shook his head.

"Listen, Your Highness," said Annie. "I'm stuck in this tower and I need to get out. Do you think you could come back tomorrow with a ladder or whatever you need to get me down from here?"

"Actually, I have plans with my wife tomorrow. Thursday is my day to visit Rapunzel. We've had a standing appointment for years."

Annie laughed to herself. "This just gets better and better. Did Rapunzel know that you're married?" she called down to the young man.

"The subject never came up," he said, sounding stiff and angry. "It's obvious that I'm wasting my time here," he added, and turned to walk away.

"Wait!" called Annie. "If you happen to see a young man named Liam, please tell him that Princess Annie is in this tower and needs to be rescued!"

"Rescue yourself!" Prince Ludlow shouted back. Dashing the flowers to the ground, he stalked back to where he'd tied up his horse.

"That's exactly what I'm trying to do," Annie murmured as she returned to the chair and picked up the hair rope again.

Annie worked on the braid for the rest of the day, and went to sleep that night with only a little more to do. Excited and nervous, she didn't sleep well and got up as the first rays of the sun peeped over the ledge of the easternmost window. It didn't take long for her to finish the braid, knotting the end in a circle just big enough for her foot.

The braid was as thick as two of her fingers and held up well when she tested it, so she tied her own hair back, hitched up her skirts, and carried the rope to the table. Running the rope around a table leg, she stuck her foot in the circle she'd made and wrapped the braid around her waist, just as Liam had taught her to do outside the ogre's castle. Then, perched on the windowsill, she dangled her legs over the edge and dropped the other end of the braid. It fell in a golden coil, unfurling down the side of the tower until the end lay draped across the ground.

Annie swallowed hard. The ground looked far away now. If she were to slip or make a wrong move... Resolving not to look down again, she grasped the dangling rope with both hands and lowered herself down the wall. The first few yards went well, but her arms soon began to shake and she had to force herself to keep going.

Annie was nearly halfway down when she heard a

horse and rider below her, but she didn't dare look. With her breath rasping in her throat and her heart racing, all she could do was focus on working her way hand under hand down the rope. She had nearly reached the ground when a pain of strong arms wrapped around her waist and lowered her the rest of the way.

"I thought I'd lost you for good," said a familiar voice, and Annie looked up into Liam's eyes. "Was it too terrible?" he asked, glancing up at the tower.

"You have no idea," she replied, letting her head rest against him. "So who told you where to find me— Mortimer or Ludlow?"

"Neither," he said, sounding confused. "Actually, I found the men who kidnapped you. They were happy enough to tell me where you were once I'd tied them up and offered to shorten their miserable lives."

Annie smiled, even though he couldn't see it. "You do have a way with words."

CHAPTER 14

ANNIE TURNED IN HER SADDLE to look behind her, but they had ridden far enough that she could no longer see the tower above the tops of the trees. When she was facing forward again, it occurred to her that something wasn't quite right. "Are you sure this is the way to Treecrest? The sun is in front of us. That means we're headed west."

"We're taking a short detour," said Liam. "There's another prince I want you to meet."

Annie tugged on her reins, making her horse stop short. "But I need to get to Treecrest as soon as possible. I should be there already. The princes are probably waiting for me."

"And they'll continue to wait," Liam said. He rode up beside her so that their knees were touching. Leaning across the space between them, he rested his hand on hers and squeezed it gently. Annie looked up, flustered, and felt her face redden when he looked into her eyes and added, "I swear that this is important. I wouldn't ask you to do it otherwise."

Annie had to clear her throat to speak. "How far away is this prince?"

"We'll reach his castle before dark. We can spend the night there and leave for Treecrest in the morning."

"Who is the prince?"

"His name is Clarence. He's the crown prince of Dorinocco...and he's my brother."

"You mean you feel a special kinship with him? What did he do, save your life, or did you save his?"

Liam shook his head. "Nothing like that. I mean he's my actual brother. We have to go see him, but I thought you should know who I am before we get there."

"That doesn't make sense! You were a guard in my parents' castle, and you've been guarding me for the last few days. Why would a prince pretend to be a guard? Oh, I get it! We're going to pretend that you're a prince while we're there, just like we pretended that I was a boy when we went to Shimshee."

"That's not at all what I meant," Liam said, letting go of her hand as he sat back in his saddle. "I really am a prince! I know I may not look like one, certainly not like Clarence. He's the handsome one."

"So you and Clarence are like Gwennie and me? One of you got all the magic gifts and the other is normal?"

"Sort of," said Liam.

Annie nodded. "I see. It isn't that you want to pretend to be a prince now—you were pretending to be a guard all along. Congratulations. Everyone in Treecrest believed you. Why were you there? To spy on us? I feel so stupid!" She was angry, too, and the more she thought about how close they'd become and how much she'd trusted him, the madder she grew.

"I wasn't there to spy on you!" said Liam. "My intentions were never anything but good."

"Really?" said Annie. "Then why didn't you tell us the truth?"

"Because I couldn't," Liam replied. "I wanted to tell you. Lying to you was one of the hardest things I've ever done." He looked so sincere and earnest that Annie found herself wanting to believe him. But if he hadn't told her who he really was, what else hadn't he told her?

৵

Annie thought the castle was beautiful. Located on the top of a high hill, it offered its occupants an uninterrupted view of the surrounding countryside. It was riddled with so many slender towers and swooping archways that the entire white-stone structure looked light enough to float away. Even the gates were a sparkling white and looked as fragile as lace. Annie could hear their magic singing as she passed below them. Curious, she reached out a tentative hand and touched the white metal, which immediately turned a dull gray. She had thought the magic made them strong, but it really just masked their true appearance.

Liam rode ahead of her to speak with the guards by the steps leading into the castle keep, and though she couldn't hear what they said, she saw them bow their heads in deference before one of them turned and hurried into the castle. When the prince dismounted, stable boys rushed to take his horse's reins.

Liam's manner had changed as they'd approached the castle, and he now had the regal bearing of a prince, with his back straight and his head held high. He came to help Annie down from her horse, looking as if he wanted to say something, but a young man in his late teens arrived, distracting them both. He was one of the most handsome men Annie had ever seen, with hair the color of sunlight and vivid blue eyes that reminded her more than a little of her sister's.

"Liam!" said the young man. "Where have you been? I was hoping we'd seen the last of you, but Father has been talking about sending out a search party. He's been waiting for you to return ever since—"

"Clarence," Liam interrupted, "I'd like you to meet Princess Annabelle of Treecrest, the second daughter to King Halbert and Queen Karolina." Taking Annie's hand in his, Liam led her toward the young man.

"Whatever possessed you to bring her here?"

demanded an older woman, who had followed Prince Clarence out the door.

"I have my reasons," Liam said. "Annie, this is my mother, Queen Lenore. I thought it was time you met."

"You'd better have a good explanation," said the queen, and she turned to go back into the castle.

Annie held Liam's hand as he escorted her inside, glancing at him out of the corner of her eyes now and then. She saw the guarded way he looked at his mother and brother, and thought it would be better not to try to talk to him again as long as they were around. Following the queen up the steps and down a long, airy corridor, they entered the Great Hall. Two wooden statues of armed soldiers flanked the door with other statues standing at attention below the tapestries that hung on the walls. It was an impressive room and far grander than the Great Hall in Treecrest.

The queen stopped at a table and pointed at the bench beside it. "You will wait here," she ordered Annie. "I wish to speak with my son alone."

The queen's manner would have been enough to make Annie dislike her, but she liked the woman even less when she saw the look of scorn she cast at Liam. Annie didn't think any mother should look at her son that way. She felt a pang of sympathy for him as she watched him leave the Hall.

"I wouldn't want to be him right now," said Clarence. "Mother doesn't like surprises. There must be more to you than meets the eye if he was willing to bring you here. You don't look like much, certainly not like any princess I've ever met."

"Really? You look like a typical prince."

Clarence scowled, just like Gwennie would have if anyone had said that she was less than extraordinary. Annie had to stop herself from smiling; the prince was so much like her sister that she felt as if she already knew him.

"I don't care what you say; she is a true princess and deserves to be treated like one," Liam said from the door to the Great Hall. He and his mother had returned and neither one looked happy.

"Then she'll sleep in the Princess Chamber," said the queen. "It's still ready from the last time a so-called princess visited, so we won't have to go to any extra effort."

"How thoughtful of you, Mother," said Liam. His mother didn't seem to recognize the sarcasm, however.

"You know I always have my boys' best wishes at heart," she said, beaming at Clarence.

"Yes, I'm well aware of that," Liam said, glancing at Clarence as well. "Annie," he called, seeing her seated at the table. "We have much to talk about."

"Not tonight, you won't," Queen Lenore snapped. "The girl is going to the chamber now. You can talk to her in the morning and then I'll send her on her way."

Annie was dismayed. She wanted time alone to talk to Liam. She had so many questions that she wasn't sure where to begin. Why had he pretended to be a guard? Why had he brought her here? Why was his mother acting as if she didn't believe Annie was a real princess? Why was Prince Clarence sneering at her again? Did she really want someone like him to contend for her sister's hand?

The queen tilted her head back so that she was looking down her nose when she finally addressed Annie. "My son insists that you are a true princess and deserving of every courtesy. Therefore, you will be shown to the chamber we reserve for visiting princesses, where you will remain until morning. At that time, I will decide on what course of action we will take next.

"You!" the queen declared, pointing at one of the guards. "Take this girl to the Princess Chamber and make sure that she stays there until I send for her in the morning. And as for you," she said, turning back to Liam, "our conversation is not over yet!"

The Princess Chamber was partway down a long corridor where the last rays of the setting sun slipped through a tall, narrow window at the far end, providing the only light. Annie was listening for magic when the guard stopped and opened one of the many doors. She had scarcely stepped over the threshold when the door shut behind her and she heard the locking bolt grate home.

Annie frowned. She didn't like being locked up anywhere, especially after spending so many days imprisoned inside a tower. Hoping to find a second door or some other way to get out, Annie began inspecting the room. Floor-to-ceiling wall hangings divided the front of the room from the back. A small gilded table and three uncomfortable chairs stood on one side of the door, while a tall cupboard rested against the wall on the other. Candelabrum scattered around the room held a wealth of tapered candles. Annie expected to see a normal bed on the other side of the curtain, but when she pushed her way through she was surprised to find a stack of mattresses rising higher than her head.

"They've got to be joking!" Annie muttered as she walked around the mattresses, inspecting them from every side. "That woman is crazy if she thinks I'm going to sleep up there." The mattresses smelled musty and their edges were speckled with mildew. They had obviously been there for a very long time.

The sound of the door scraping open drew Annie back through the curtains to the other side of the room. A maid was setting food on the gilded table. She was laying a rose beside the plate when she looked up and saw Annie. "Good evening, Your Highness. My name is Meg. I've brought you your supper. The rose is from Prince Liam. He said to tell you that he's sorry, although he didn't tell me what for."

"Thank you," said Annie. "And please thank Liam for me. And while you're at it, tell him that I can't possibly sleep on top of a pile of mattresses. I don't even know how I'd get up there."

"That's easy enough," said Meg, who looked to be about the same age as Annie. "There's a ladder. Here, I'll help you set it up."

Annie followed the girl back through the curtain to where a long wooden ladder lay on the floor under the only window in the room. Metal bars crisscrossed the window, making it impossible to get out that way.

Pushing up her sleeves, Meg reached for the ladder. "Here you go," she said as she lugged it to the side of the mattresses. "Now you can sleep up there snug as a bug in a rug."

Annie poked one of the mattresses with her finger. A puff of dust wafted toward her face. Coughing, she wiped her eyes with her sleeve. "I can't sleep on a stinky old pile of mattresses! You can tell the queen that I said—"

"Oh, but Your Highness, you have to!" said the girl, her eyes opening wide. "The queen expects you to, and if you don't she'll take it out on me!"

"I won't tell her if you won't," said Annie. "All I need is a blanket and I'll be able to sleep down here. This floor can't be any worse than the one I slept on for the last few nights."

"Please don't, Your Highness! What if the queen walks in during the night and sees that you're not on the mattresses?"

"I suppose she might...," said Annie.

"Surely you can sleep up there for just one night?" the girl added.

Annie sighed. "I guess so..."

"Good! Then it's all settled. I'll be back with a fresh tray in the morning. In the meantime, just call out if you need me. I'm to sleep right outside your door." The girl smiled as she extinguished most of the candles before bustling out of the room, leaving Annie looking up at the mattresses.

She was testing the first rung of the ladder with her foot when the scent of roast chicken lured her to the table by the door. Although everything looked delicious, the rich, heavy sauces coating the chicken, peas, and baby potatoes kept her from sampling more than a few bites. After a small sip of wine, she set down the goblet. Something must be wrong with her; everything tasted like the herb her nanny had used to help her sleep when she was young. *Maybe,* she thought, *the moldy cheese I ate in the tower makes everything taste funny.*

It was dark outside the window when Annie finally climbed the ladder, counting each mattress as she passed it. "Twenty, twenty-one, twenty-two... There are twenty-two mattresses here, and I bet Queen Lenore didn't give me even one decent pillow. For someone who acts like she thinks she's better than everyone, Liam's mother is a lousy hostess."

Annie was surprised when she reached the top, however. The highest mattress was filled with down and covered with a blanket as soft and warm as kitten fur. There were three pillows on the bed, each one stuffed with down that poofed out around her head when she tested it. The pillows and blanket all smelled like lavender, a scent she'd always found relaxing.

Yawning, Annie snuggled under the covers and closed her eyes. She was exhausted and expected to fall asleep right away and so was surprised to find herself still awake a few minutes later. She changed her position, hoping that would make a difference, then stared into the dark as the last flickering candle went out. She moved her legs from one side of the bed to the other. She rolled over and tried sleeping on her other side. She plumped up her pillows, wadded them into balls, and pounded them with her fist. No matter how she positioned herself, she couldn't get comfortable.

Annie willed herself to relax, forcing every part of her to go limp, starting with her eyebrows. She tried to think about something pleasant, but wound up thinking about Liam. She thought about all the angry, hurtful things she'd like to say to him for lying to her about being a guard, getting tenser with each passing second. When she realized what she was doing, she had to force herself to relax all over again. She thought about how much Liam had helped her and how, aside from lying about his identity, he had shown that he had more integrity than most of the men she'd met. Lying there in the dark, she decided that Liam had earned the right to be heard; whatever he had to say, it had better be good.

She rolled over again and flung her arms wide.

Maybe she'd never go to sleep again. Maybe she'd forgotten how.

Annie was lying on her back with her legs dangling over the side of the mattresses when the music began. The lute music was soft and soothing, as was the voice that sang the lullaby. It was a tune that had never failed to put her to sleep when she was a baby. Now, in the middle of the night when she was trying to sleep, she found it irritating. She sat up and listened. It sounded as if the music was coming from right outside her door.

Annie flopped back on the bed and pulled the ends of a pillow up around her ears. When that didn't work, she turned on her side and pulled the pillow over her head, leaving just enough space to breathe. She could still hear the music.

The first tune ended and the unseen musician began another. "No!" Annie shouted, yanking the pillow off the bed and pitching it at the curtain. "Stop playing! People are trying to sleep around here!"

The music stopped abruptly. For a moment, Annie thought she heard the murmur of voices. When all she could hear was silence, she lay back down, hoping that maybe now she could finally go to sleep. Yet even as tired as she was, Annie still found it impossible to get comfortable. She rolled over again, but this time she was too close to the edge and nearly fell off. Feeling nothing but air under half her body, she rolled back and lay still, clinging to the mattress.

Annie was lying on her back, her eyes wide open, when the first rays of sunlight grayed the darkness of night. She knew that if she sat up, she could reach out and touch the ceiling, but that would mean moving limbs that felt like dead weights. Annie dozed then, coming fully awake when her door creaked open.

"Is that you, Meg?" Annie called, not sure if she'd slept for even a moment.

"It's me, Your Highness," Meg replied. "Queen Lenore wants you to come to break your fast with her if you're awake."

"I'm awake, all right," Annie said, sounding grim. "Just like I've been all night."

Although she expected to return to the Great Hall, Annie followed Meg to a much smaller chamber. A round table had been set up at one end of the room. Queen Lenore was there, with her two sons flanking her on either side. An older man was seated across from the queen. His leg was propped on a cushion and he wore a soft slipper on his foot.

"Come here, girl," said Queen Lenore, gesturing to her with an imperious wave of her hand.

Liam frowned at his mother and said, "Her name is Princess Annabelle."

"Humph," said the queen. "So how did you sleep, my

dear?" she asked Annie. "Tell the truth now. I'll know if you're lying."

"I slept very poorly," said the old man. "If anyone is interested."

Annie yawned and wiped her eyes, which refused to stop tearing. "I didn't sleep at all," she replied. "I couldn't get comfortable on your mattress tower."

"I don't believe you. Someone told you to say that," said the queen, glaring at Liam.

"Don't look at me," Liam replied. "I haven't spoken to Annie since you sent her off to that room. Tell me," he said, turning to Annie, "is the tower of mattresses still as tall?"

"I counted twenty-two," said Annie. "I could touch the ceiling when I sat up. Why did I have to sleep on all those mattresses anyway?"

"My mother has a theory," Liam began. "She thinks that a real princess would be so sensitive that she couldn't sleep if there was so much as a pea under her mattress. She tests every girl who claims to be a princess."

The queen looked as if she was thinking about something else entirely, so Annie asked Liam, "Why would she doubt them?"

"She doesn't think any princess is really a princess. It's because she doesn't think any girl is good enough for Clarence. Plus, she likes to torment whomever she can."

Annie stifled another yawn. "But I don't understand—wouldn't a mattress squash a pea? Then it would be flat and no one would feel it."

Liam chuckled and said in a loud whisper, "I doubt Mother thought of that. She doesn't have much of an imagination."

Queen Lenore shot Liam a disgusted look. Holding her nose even higher in the air, she gestured to a guard, saying, "You, come here." After speaking to the queen for a moment, the guard hurried from the room.

"I'm going to watch the troops drill today," said the old man. "I can't ride a horse anymore, but I can keep my leg up if I go in one of the carriages. Liam, why don't you join me? Your brother has never been interested in anything military."

"I'd like to, but I have to escort the princess home."

"Very good, my boy. Very good. I taught you to be chivalrous and I'm pleased to see that you learned your lessons well."

Everyone looked up as the guard reentered the room along with Meg and a young man carrying a lute.

"Did you sleep outside the door of the Princess Chamber as I commanded you to last night?" Queen Lenore asked Meg.

Meg bobbed up and down in a quick curtsey. "Yes, Your Highness. After I took the princess's supper to her, no one went in and no one came out."

"Did you hear her snore or make any other sound that would indicate she was asleep?"

"No, Your Highness. All I heard was a lovely lullaby." Meg smiled at the young man with the lute.

"Have you seen Liam's carvings?" the old man asked Annie. "He whittled a unicorn for me when he was just a boy. Here it is. I had a pocket made especially for it. It's six inches tall, but it looks so real, doesn't it? He carved those statues in the Great Hall, too. Although the wooden soldiers are larger than life, the weapons' proportions are the same as the real ones."

"They're very impressive," said Annie. She was so tired that she had to fight to stay awake.

"As for you," the queen said, turning to the lute player. "Did you play the lullabies as I ordered you to?"

"Yes," said the young man. "I played until the princess told me to stop."

Queen Lenore scowled.

"I told you she was a princess," said Liam.

"Be that as it may, I still don't understand why you brought her here," said Clarence.

"Because I thought it was about time you met and that you learned about Princess Annabelle's quest. It has been my privilege to accompany her as she locates princes to kiss her sister."

"What's this?" said the old man. "Why does her sister need a kiss?"

"Father, I'm sorry no one ever introduced you and Annabelle. The lovely young lady standing before you is Princess Annabelle of Treecrest, the younger daughter of King Halbert and Queen Karolina, who are at present asleep in their castle. They will remain asleep until the day their older daughter, Princess Gwendolyn, receives a kiss from the prince who happens to be her true love. Whoever wakes the princess will win her hand in marriage, placing him in line to rule Treecrest at the side of his queen one day."

"Are you saying that if Clarence kisses this girl, she'll marry him and he'll be the next ruler of Treecrest?" asked the queen.

"If he wakes her, yes."

Queen Lenore looked indignant. "Of course she'd wake if Clarence kissed her. He's the most eligible prince in all the known kingdoms."

"And Princess Gwendolyn is known to be the most beautiful princess. Even now princes are thronging to the castle, eager to win her hand."

"They are?" the queen said, aghast.

"I should go, Mother," Clarence said, getting to his feet.

The queen held up her hand as if to stop him. "But all our preparations..."

"What preparations?" asked the king.

"Those preparations have been very expensive," said

Clarence. "A prolonged campaign would be even more costly. However, if I were to win the princess's hand in front of all those princes..."

"No one could deny your right to rule!" exclaimed the queen. "Brilliant, my dear boy."

"What preparations?" the king asked again. "What have you been up to, Lenore?"

"I think it's time for us to go, Annie," said Liam. "I'll have the cook pack some food to take with us."

"As much as I hate going anywhere with you, we might as well ride together if we're going to the same place," Clarence told Liam.

"Great!" Liam muttered under his breath.

"Pardon me?" his brother said, raising one eyebrow.

"That's great!" Liam said more loudly. Clarence looked satisfied and went off to collect his things.

Annie covered her mouth as she yawned again, wishing that she had the time to take a nice long nap.

CHAPTER 15

ANNIE WAITED IN THE GREAT HALL while Liam and Clarence prepared for the trip ahead. She stood to the side, out of the way and unnoticed, only half watching the whirl of activity. Exhausted, she would have fallen asleep standing up if her mind weren't thrumming with unasked questions, most of which would have to wait until she and Liam were alone.

Annie didn't like the thought of traveling with Clarence. She had a lot of questions for Liam, and had no desire to discuss any of them in front of Clarence. In addition, she and Liam had established their own routines and recognized each other's moods; anyone traveling with them was bound to change things. And from what she had seen of Clarence, he was as self-centered as most of the princes she'd met, unlike Liam. For a moment she wondered how two brothers could be so different, and if it had anything to do with magic the way it had in her own family. Liam was handsome, but not overwhelmingly so, while Clarence looked too good to be real, like an artist's idealized portrait of what a handsome man should be.

She was musing about what it might have been like to grow up in Liam's family when Clarence entered the Hall. When he didn't seem to see her, she shrank back against the wall, not wanting to have to talk to him without Liam around. A moment later his mother appeared and strode directly to Clarence. Mother and son spoke briefly, then the queen tucked what looked like a piece of parchment under the flap of Clarence's saddlebag, kissed him on the cheek, and left.

Liam arrived shortly after and spotted Annie right away. Smiling, he waved and hurried over to talk to her. "Everything is ready," he said, showing her his stuffed saddlebag.

"Good," said Annie. "I should have returned to Treecrest days ago. How long will the trip take us?"

"Almost two days," said Liam.

"That long? I suppose it's just as well. I need to talk to you about a lot of things."

"I know," said Liam, his smile fading. "I apologize in advance for most of what you're going to say."

"There you are," said Clarence, motioning to the servant carrying his saddlebag. "How many servants are you taking?"

"None," said Liam. "And neither are you. An entourage would hold us back and we don't have time for that."

"That's preposterous!" spluttered Clarence. "Every prince needs an entourage when he travels."

"Let him take one, Liam," said Annie. "We'll go now and he can follow with his servants. It shouldn't take more than a day or two extra before he joins us. By that time all the princes who are already there will have kissed Gwennie. Since they've all hurried to reach her side, one of them is bound to be her true love."

"Never mind," said Clarence, taking his saddlebag from his servant. "I suppose I can rough it if you can."

"Too bad," Liam said, and winked at Annie.

❧

They were out in the courtyard when Liam saw that she was struggling to keep her eyes open. "You're riding with me," he said, boosting her onto the back of the stallion he was to ride. "The last thing we need is for you to go to sleep and get hurt when you fall off your horse." After settling on the saddle behind Annie, he reached around her to grip the reins.

"This is nice," she murmured, snuggling into his arms.

"What did you say?" Liam asked, but Annie was already asleep.

She dozed as she rode tucked against Liam's chest and didn't wake while they clattered across the drawbridge and down the main road. They were passing through a village when she woke, still tired, but not nearly as much as she had been. They traveled straight through for most of the day, stopping to stretch their legs only once when Clarence's complaints grew too loud. By midafternoon he was dawdling, so they rode ahead after telling him that they were going to make sure the way was safe. Annie was relieved when they could no longer see Clarence behind them and she and Liam were finally alone.

"Before we talk about anything else," said Annie, "I need to know why you lied to me. Why did you pretend to be a guard?"

"Because I wanted to protect you," said Liam. "Would you have let me come with you if you'd known I hadn't told the truth when I got the job in your parents' castle? I'm not in the habit of lying. I never would have if I hadn't thought you needed me."

"But why did you lie in the first place? Why get a job in my parents' castle at all? Normally I'd think it was so you could be close to Gwennie. Our last steward came to work there for that very reason. My father had him banished from the kingdom when he learned that the man had been following Gwennie around and spying on her. But you weren't like that. I never saw you pay her any special attention."

"I wasn't there because of your sister, or at least not the way you think. I had overheard something I wasn't supposed to hear and—"

"Wait for me!" Clarence shouted from behind them.

His horse's breathing was labored when he rode up, making Annie wonder just how far back he'd been before he decided to join them.

"I don't suppose there's an inn up ahead," said Clarence. "Somewhere clean where we can spend the night. I want a bath and a good hot meal."

"There aren't any inns on this stretch of road," said Liam.

Clarence scowled. "You made us come this way just to torment me, didn't you? Mother always said I shouldn't trust you."

"Did she now?" Liam replied. "And I thought you and Mother were the ones I couldn't trust. I heard how you were trying to embroil our family in the most under-handed, deceitful—"

"Mother was right," Clarence said, his lip curled in a sneer. "You don't care anything about Dorinocco. We've been planning strategy because we want to make our kingdom the greatest power in all the land, but you're too interested in 'doing the right thing' to do what *needs* to be done. You'll see—when I become king of Treecrest, profit from linder tree fabric will fill Dorinocco's coffers. You and Father will get to play soldier, but only because of me."

"What you call planning strategy most people call sneaking around and plotting behind the king's back.

Father won't be happy when he learns the full extent of what you and Mother have done."

Clarence's eyes narrowed as he leaned forward in his saddle. "And I suppose you plan to tell him...if you haven't already."

"I don't need to. Father already suspects that you're up to something. It won't be long before he's uncovered it all."

"By then I'll be married to the princess Gwendolyn and it won't matter."

"We'll see," said Liam. "You're not the only prince going to Treecrest who thinks he'll win her hand. I know you and Mother don't doubt that you'll wake her, but I don't think you're good enough to be her true love. Being handsome isn't everything."

Clarence scowled at his brother. "You always were a sniveling little—"

"I don't agree," Liam said, shaking his head. "I'm taller than you by a good four inches and I haven't sniveled since I was a baby. You, on the other hand, have been whiny your whole life."

Clarence's knuckles were white from gripping the reins when he kicked the sides of his horse and took off at a gallop.

"Ouch!" said Annie as Clarence disappeared down the road. "I guess you two *really* don't get along."

"We never have," Liam replied. "But I blame my mother more than anyone." He sighed and shifted in his seat. "Clarence was my parents' firstborn and Mother thought he was very special. When he was about to be christened, Mother nagged the local fairies into giving him every gift she could think of relating to good looks and social graces. When I was born, the fairies resented her earlier demands so much that most of them stayed away from my christening. Unlike most princes, I don't have a magically enhanced appearance, I'm not the best dancer in the kingdom, and I couldn't write poetry if my life depended on it. By the way, I very much liked the poem you recited for Andreas's contest."

Annie grinned. "Thank you. There was no magic involved in that, either."

"I know, which is why it was so great. Anyway, Clarence was handsome and gifted, while I was ordinary, at least according to my mother. She reminded me of this every time I failed to meet her expectations, which was most of the time. I was happiest when Mother ignored me, and I spent more time with my father than most princes spend with theirs. He taught me how to shoot an arrow and wield a sword before I reached the age of nine. Father decided that I should learn all the manly arts; if he couldn't teach me something himself, he found someone who could."

"Your father seems like a very nice man," said Annie.

"He is nice, and that's something no one can say about my mother. She likes to manipulate people, although she's never been able to control my father. Clarence was a different story, however. He's been under her thumb his whole life. I'd almost feel sorry for him, except I think he enjoys it so much. Being her favorite son meant that he got whatever he wanted and could pick on me without fear of retaliation. They're two of a kind, and it's not a kind I like. Mother has goals for Clarence that exceed simply ruling Dorinocco."

Annie nodded. "I saw how excited she became when she thought he could marry Gwennie and rule Treecrest as well. But it's not unusual for parents to have big dreams for their children."

"It's not the dreaming that's a problem," said Liam. "It's how people go about achieving the dreams that concerns me."

"So why didn't you tell your father about Clarence and your mother when you saw him?"

Liam sighed. "I probably should have, but I thought I could deal with this myself. He looks so frail now...I want to make his life easier when I can. If I had my way, he'd never have to learn about any of this, but he's probably already ferreted out most of the details now that he knows something is going on. Look, there's Clarence. I suppose it was too much to hope that he would go on without us. He's probably going to tell us that he wants to stop for the night, even though there are hours of daylight left."

"Do you have any idea where you want to stay the night?"

"I do indeed. We'll stop when I can't stand Clarence's whining anymore."

"Pretty soon then, huh?" Annie said.

Liam laughed and shook his head. "You'd be surprised how much I've learned to put up with."

A few hours later they set up camp in a copse of trees just off the main road. Together, Annie and Liam watered the horses at a nearby stream and built a campfire from fallen twigs. Before they could ask him to help, Clarence announced that he was going to look for berries and wandered off. He came back just as Liam was serving the food the cook had packed, then sat by himself to eat. When he finished eating, he took his bedroll and disappeared among the trees.

"Your brother isn't very social, is he?" said Annie as she helped Liam clean up after supper.

"Not when he's around me. He knows I'm not as easily impressed as the courtiers who follow him like lapdogs, so he doesn't bother trying."

Annie glanced at the woods in the direction Clarence had gone. "He knows about me, doesn't he? I saw the way he looks at me, and he avoids touching me altogether. He nearly tripped over his own feet backing away from me when I tried to hand him his plate earlier."

Liam nodded without looking at her. "He knows."

"Your mother does, too, I bet. Did you notice that none of them asked why my parents were asleep or why I wasn't asleep as well? Word must have gotten out already.

229

Listen, I want to go wash up before it's too dark to see. I'll be right back so we can talk."

"You'd better take a torch with you," Liam suggested. "There might be snakes in the brush."

"Good thinking," said Annie, taking the one he offered. She held the torch high as she made her way to the stream, and was glad she had it when she returned. It was darker then, with clouds scudding across the night sky, blocking the light of the waning moon.

She was passing the tethered horses on her way back to the campsite when she noticed something white on the ground. Curious, she bent down and picked up a folded piece of parchment. Holding the torch with one hand, she unfolded the parchment with the other. Something shiny fell out, landing at her feet. Once again Annie bent down, and this time she picked up a pin. "How odd," she murmured, and turned her attention back to the parchment. It was the note that Queen Lenore had handed to Clarence.

As a rule, Annie didn't read other people's letters, but this time curiosity got the better of her and she held the note up to the light of the torch.

My Dearest Clarence –
If the kiss doesn't work, wake the princess in whatever
way you can. Slap her, jab her with a pin (which I've
enclosed), pull her hair, bite her lip . . . Do what you
need to, but get her to open her eyes, even if it's for only a

second. They never said she had to stay awake. If Liam and that girl Annie deny that you are Gwendolyn's true love, we can always claim that they went back on their word and get the neighboring kingdoms behind us. Don't worry, my darling boy. You'll get that throne yet!
Love, Mother

Annie was horrified. To think that someone would want to cheat like that, and to do it by stabbing her sister with a pin! With a flick of her fingers, Annie dropped the pin and ground it into the dirt with the toe of her shoe. She glanced back at the note. The words that the queen had written were bad enough, but there was something about the handwriting...Annie gasped and crushed the note in her hand. She'd recognized the handwriting with its curlicues and flourishes—it was the same as the writing on the note that had come with the tiny jeweled spinning wheel on which her sister had pricked her finger.

Liam looked up from his seat beside the campfire as Annie came storming back. Her hand shook as she thrust the note in his face, saying, "Your mother was the one who sent the jeweled spinning wheel! She's the one who made my sister fall asleep. It was your family's fault that my family is in this mess! You want to take over our kingdom! That's why you got a job in my parents' castle. You *were* there to spy on us!"

Liam shook his head. "I had no part in my mother's

plan. I learned about her intentions after she had already set everything in motion. I got the job as a guard so I could stop her. I was trying to protect your family!"

"Why should I believe you?"

"Because it's the truth," he said, reaching for her hand. "I've been trying to keep you safe all along and you know it. From the moment I realized that you'd escaped from the castle, I've done everything I could to protect you. I *want* you to find the prince who can wake your sister. I want your entire family to wake up!"

Suddenly Annie no longer had the energy to argue. She sank down onto the log beside Liam and rested her head in her hands. "Tell me about the plot you mentioned."

"I overheard my mother talking to Clarence one day. She had hired an old witch to take a spinning wheel to the castle to send Gwendolyn into a deep sleep. Father's leg was paining him more than usual and he'd shut himself away in his chamber, so I decided that it was up to me to stop them. I went to Treecrest to find the witch, hoping I could handle it without anyone else learning what they had done. I was relieved when you got rid of her, and I thought the danger was over, otherwise I never would have gone on the captain of the guard's errand. I wasn't gone long, but when I came back and found the wall of roses, I knew that I'd heard only part of my mother's plan. I didn't know about the other spinning wheel until you told me about it."

"You mean that errand was real? You didn't make it up so you could leave before my sister pricked her finger?"

"It was very real. I already told you, I don't like lying!"

"I'm sorry," Annie said, her lips so stiff that it was hard to speak. "Please continue."

"There's not much else to tell. I tried to get into the castle, but the roses were everywhere. I stayed around hoping I'd find a secret way in. My parents' castle has at least two, so I thought yours might as well. I made three circuits around the castle and even checked for under-water entrances on the river side. I was in the woods starting another circuit when I found some of my mother's men. I watched them until I knew they couldn't get in, either. Then I saw your footprints and tracked you to the woods where I found you."

"So Clarence knows about your mother's plan?"

"As far as I know, he was in on it from the beginning."

Annie had decided to trust Liam before. It was even harder to trust him now, but part of her still wanted to. "So what do we do?"

Liam relaxed, almost as if his entire body had been tense until he knew that she believed him. "We do exactly what we're already doing. I took you to see Clarence and my mother when I did for a couple of reasons. When I found those men who kidnapped you, I recognized them as some who worked for my mother. She had you kid-napped and locked in the tower to keep you out of the way while she took over Treecrest. I wanted her to back off, so I thought it was time we went to see her. Mother and Clarence needed to know about the other princes. Clarence wouldn't dare try to take over the kingdom by trickery with so many royals there. I wanted him to stop what he was planning long enough that we could reach the castle without his men waylaying us.

"They won't have their soldiers try anything now since they're both convinced that Clarence is going to wake Gwendolyn and win her hand. My mother has to know that Clarence's marriage to your sister would be a much better way to take over the kingdom. Fighting costs lives and money. It might also lead to the destruction of linder trees. If Clarence were to wake Gwendolyn, at least he would have gotten control through honest means, but I doubt very much that that will happen. If someone else kisses her and your family wakes up, Clarence will have to call his men back. Once he returns home, Father's going to be furious. He's tried to maintain peaceful relations with the neighboring kingdoms for his entire reign, and despite what Mother and Clarence seem to think, my father is still in charge."

"But what if my family doesn't wake up?"

"Am I right in assuming that anyone who isn't touching you will fall asleep?" said Liam. When Annie nodded, he continued, saying, "Then we leave Clarence to sleep along with everyone else in the castle, and keep looking until we find Gwendolyn's true love. Don't worry, if this doesn't work, we're not giving up."

"Thank you!" Annie said, her words so heartfelt that tears made her eyes glisten.

"Don't thank me yet," said Liam. "We have a lot to do tomorrow and no guarantee that any of it will come out right."

Suddenly there was crashing in the forest and two figures emerged from behind a tree. Liam leaped to his feet and reached for his crossbow, but Annie just leaned forward for a better look. "Is that you, Beldegard?" she called. "What are you doing with Clarence?"

The bear prince lumbered closer, dragging Clarence by the collar. When he reached the light of the campfire, Beldegard pinned the prince to the ground with one massive paw and spit out the collar with a loud *ptew!* "I found this dreg of humanity lurking behind a tree, listening in on your conversation. Do you want me to eat him for you, or what?"

"Get your paws off me, you flea-bitten bear rug! I'm Prince Clarence of Dorinocco and I have every right to be here. I'm traveling with my brother and the princess."

"But you didn't have any right to listen in on a private conversation," said Liam. "How long were you there?"

"Long enough to hear that you plan to leave me in the castle, asleep! Wait until Mother hears this!"

"And I thought my family has problems!" said

Beldegard. "I take it you wouldn't want your mother to hear about that nap you have planned for sneaky boy here?"

"It would be better if she didn't," said Liam.

"Then I'll see to it that he doesn't go anywhere. I owe you one, Princess. I found those children you told me about and I took them to the widow's cottage. That's when I saw the woman I'd intended to marry kissing another man."

"I'm so sorry to hear that!" said Annie.

"Yeah, and I was sorry to see it, but I'm glad I found out now instead of after the wedding. I wouldn't want to marry someone who didn't love me, now would I?"

"Why would a girl want to marry a bear?" asked Clarence.

The bear cuffed him across the head, making Clarence duck when the bear raised his paw again. "I'm an enchanted prince, you dunderhead!" roared Beldegard. "Didn't you notice that I can talk?"

"Now that you mention it ..."

"We're on our way to Treecrest," said Annie. "You're welcome to join us if you'd like."

"We are inviting princes, after all," said Liam.

"I might as well," said the bear prince. "I lost track of that dwarf days ago and haven't seen him since." Raising his paw, he gestured to Annie and Liam. "You two go ahead and get some sleep. I don't need much sleep this time of year, so I'll keep an eye on this fella...Hey you, come back here!"

Clarence had taken advantage of Beldegard's raised paw to roll out of reach and stand up. In only three steps, the bear prince had knocked him down again. "I'd go to sleep, too, if I were you," he growled into Clarence's ear. "I said I wasn't sleepy, but I never said I wasn't hungry! Say good night to your brother and the princess."

"Good night, everyone," Clarence hurried to say.

"Excellent," said Beldegard. "I think we're going to get along just fine."

CHAPTER 16

FOR ALL THE TRAVELING Annie had done, she thought that the last few miles to Treecrest were the longest. Since Beldegard had taken on the job of watching over Clarence, Annie and Liam no longer had to keep track of him. The bear prince had to stay well back from Clarence, however, because even the smallest glimpse or the faintest whiff of his bearish scent terrified the horses. Clarence had tried to get away only once. Although Annie hadn't seen what happened, she heard Beldegard roar, the horse scream, then silence. Clarence disappeared for a few minutes, but when he returned he looked chastened and not at all eager to try again.

Annie had expected the princes to be waiting by the castle gate, but she never expected so many people to be there. A group of villagers greeted her first, tossing flowers in her path when they saw that it was indeed their own beloved princess. She saw soldiers then, a few who had been out on patrol when Gwendolyn fell asleep, some who had been on leave to visit their families, and a few she didn't recognize, but Liam said they were wearing the colors of the princes who were supposed to be there. Regardless of their allegiance, however, they all saluted the brave princess who had gone on a quest to save her family and her kingdom.

She saw the princes next. Digby was there, half-drunk and declaring that he was the only one with the right to kiss the princess. His hands and face were scratched as if he'd tried to pass through the roses. Andreas greeted her with a kiss on the cheek and a bouquet of the roses that guarded the castle. Cozwald waved hello with one hand and held the hand of the little girl Clara with the other. Tomas was there as well, standing beside his father, Emilio. Annie hugged the children and greeted each of the princes with enthusiasm; she was grateful that they were there, but all the while she was hoping that they were enough, that one of them really would prove to be Gwendolyn's true love.

"Are you ready, Princess?" asked Andreas when the princes had gathered around her.

Annie took a deep breath and glanced at all the expectant faces. "No time like the present," she said, and reached for Liam's hand. "I'm going to take you in all at once. You should stay awake as long as you keep in touch with each other and with me."

"She means you hold hands," growled Beldegard, shoving Clarence toward the other princes.

Although Digby and Clarence complained, the rest of the princes hurried to get in line and take each other's hands. When Digby saw that he would be last, he ran to the front of the line and shoved Liam aside. Taking Annie's hand, he looked down at her and smiled. "Thought you'd pull a fast one, didn't you? You've never liked me and I've never liked you, but we both know that I'm the one to marry your sister. Hurry up and take me in there. I want to get this over and done."

Annie gritted her teeth and looked away. If there was one prince she wished she could ban from the castle, it would be Digby.

"I'd be nicer to Princess Annabelle if I were you," Liam said in a soft voice. Annie glanced back and was surprised to see him examining a knife as if to check its sharpness. "She means a lot to me, if you know what I mean."

"Yes. Yes, I suppose I do," Digby said, his voice coming out higher than normal. Clearing his throat he added, "And your name is…?"

"I'm Prince Liam and I'm a friend of Princess Annabelle's. Anyone who doesn't treat her nicely has to answer to me."

"Oh, and um…to me as well," murmured Digby. Annie saw that he didn't look quite as handsome as he

had before he took her hand. He looked older and more careworn, with his nose red from drinking and his hair turning limp and a dull shade of brown. His bloodshot eyes seemed to draw closer together even as she watched.

"Good!" said Liam. "Then take my hand so we can get started. Annie, are you ready?" Liam asked, looking past the prince to where Annie stood, openmouthed.

Annie closed her mouth with a snap. "Yes, as soon as your brother gets in line. Clarence, are you coming?" Annie called. "We're about to start."

"He's coming," growled Beldegard. "Even if I have to carry him in myself."

Annie waited while Clarence joined the line. She noticed that her touch changed Digby the most. As the only one she was touching directly, he was the only one who seemed to get the full effect of her non-magic. The appearance of the other princes seemed to change by varying degrees according to how close they were to her, with the ones farther away changing the least and Beldegard not changing at all. Annie wondered if the same would hold true for how well her touch kept them awake. *Well*, she thought, *if the others fall asleep, I'll just have to bring them back here, then take them in one at a time.*

With Annie leading the way, the line of princes approached the roses. She heard the faint sound of the wind chimes even before she reached the flower wall. Upon reaching the front edge of the rose wall, Annie laid her free hand gently on one of the blossoms. As if stricken with blight, the rose withered and the plant shriveled down to the ground. The roses behind it shrank back as she took one step, then another, touching a rose here and another there. She could hear the princes whispering to each other behind her; it was evident from the strain in their voices that they were afraid.

They were nearly halfway through when Annie glanced back. The roses behind them were growing again only yards from where Beldegard followed Clarence, nudging him even though the prince had nowhere to go but forward.

Their progress was slow, and it took them almost an hour to reach the drawbridge where the roses formed a solid mass, climbing from the wooden floor to the bottom of the open grate nearly a body length higher than Annie could reach. With each step she took, a swath of roses shrank back, although the taller princes still had to duck under the hanging flowers.

They had reached the last of the roses when Annie paused to look behind her once more. To her relief, all of the princes looked wide awake. "You mustn't let go, even though you may be tempted," she told the princes. "We have to walk through the keep and up to the top floor. We'll move faster now, so hold on tight."

They continued on, crossing the courtyard in an

awkward single file, and were approaching the stairs when there was a loud grunt and a thud from the back of the line. Annie turned to see Clarence beside Emilio instead of behind him. Beldegard was a few paces back, lying asleep on the ground with his nose resting on his paws.

"It looks like we have to go back," Annie said. "We're not leaving anyone behind."

All the princes groaned as she started back the way they had come.

"But why?" said Clarence. "He's just a bear."

"Would you like it if we left you behind?" Annie snapped. "You could stay here with them." She pointed at two guards who had fallen asleep leaning against a wall, neither of whom looked comfortable.

Clarence glanced at the angry faces of the other princes and turned pale. "No," he said so softly that Annie could barely hear him.

"Then stay together and don't let go, no matter whom you're touching."

As the line doubled back on itself, Annie noticed that Clarence avoided meeting anyone's eyes. He was quieter now and didn't hesitate touching Beldegard when he was close enough. The bear prince lurched to his feet, grumbling and shaking his mighty head as he lumbered after Clarence.

Once they were inside the castle, they saw sleeping people everywhere. Maids and courtiers were sprawled asleep in the halls. Pages snored softly over the boxes they had been carrying. A cat lay twitching in its sleep only feet from the sleeping mouse it had been chasing.

They climbed the stairs, quiet now as the overwhelming silence of the castle weighed down on them. Up one flight, then another, until they reached the floor where the princess Gwendolyn had her room. Once Annie crossed the threshold, the princes crowded in behind her to stare wide-eyed at the sleeping beauty.

It was Emilio who finally broke the silence, saying, "They were right. She's the most beautiful princess in all the kingdoms."

"And she's going to be my bride," said Digby, pushing Annie while dragging Liam and the rest of the princes behind him as he strode toward the bed. He was smiling when he bent down and planted a big sloppy kiss on Gwendolyn's lips. After waiting a moment, he kissed her again, harder.

When nothing happened and it looked like he was about to try again, Annie said, "That's enough. You need to stop now."

"Just one more kiss," Digby said, leaning over the princess again.

Liam tried to pull Digby away by the hand he held. When the prince refused to move, Liam looked back at Annie. "How much force do you want me to use?"

"None," she said as she let go of Digby's hand and stepped back.

All the princes closed their eyes and were asleep in an instant. Some collapsed to the floor as if made of melting ice, while the others fell against the bed, which helped to prop them up. Annie stepped around Digby and pulled on his sleeve, removing his hand from Liam's. When she took Liam's hand in hers, he and all the princes behind him woke.

"I should have made myself clear," she told the princes as they got to their feet. "If you kiss her and nothing happens, your turn is up. Please step aside then so someone else can try."

Annie and Liam moved out of the way as Andreas approached Gwendolyn. The kiss he pressed on her lips was both tender and sweet. He was obviously disappointed when nothing happened. "I suppose I could hold another contest," he said as he stepped back.

"You'll find the right girl someday," Annie said. She was disappointed, too. He would have made a pretty good brother-in-law.

Annie kept hold of Liam's hand as the other princes rearranged themselves in the line. Cozwald was the third prince to try. His kiss was so passionate that Annie had to turn away. When Gwendolyn didn't respond, Cozwald sighed and moved to stand beside Andreas. Annie had been full of anticipation just minutes before but was now starting to get nervous.

She didn't know Emilio very well, but he seemed like a nice enough person, although his experience as a frog had left him a little odd. If Gwennie married him, she'd have two stepchildren. Annie hoped that his kiss worked.

Emilio's kiss was so fast that Annie almost didn't see it. When nothing happened, he sighed and said, "Somehow, I'm not surprised." Running his hand along the linked arms so he didn't lose touch, Emilio stepped to the back of the line.

Annie didn't know what to do. Clarence was next, and she'd never expected him to be her sister's true love. They'd brought him this far only to keep him from causing trouble. If he kissed Gwennie and she actually woke up...

"It's about time!" Clarence said as the line of princes shuffled forward and he reached the side of the bed. "You should have let me go first and save all of them the trouble." He glanced at the other princes and shook his head. "None of them stood a chance." Turning to Gwendolyn, he bent over her and pressed a forceful kiss on her lips. Annie almost missed it when he pinched her sister's cheek.

"Stop that!" she said, and slapped him. "Get away from her or I'll—"

"You'll what? You wanted me to wake her didn't you?"

"Not like that! You're as awful as your brother said!"

"So that's it. You want Liam to wake her. My little brother..."

Annie reached out, jerked Liam's hand from his

246

brother's grasp and slapped it onto Beldegard's back, keeping the bear prince and the rest of the princes who were still holding hands awake. Yes, she wanted Gwennie to wake up, but Liam couldn't be her sister's true love, could he? It had never occurred to her to ask him if he wanted to kiss Gwennie, nor had he ever offered. But what if he was supposed to be with Annie's sister? Annie's heart might break, but at least the kingdom would be back to normal. Either way, it wasn't her choice to make, and if he didn't suggest it . . .

Clarence crumpled to the floor, asleep. Prince Cozwald sputtered as the bear prince sidled closer to the bed. Although Beldegard still looked quite bearlike, moving toward Annie at the head of the line had made his eyes become more human and his ears inch down his skull. "Are you going to let that beast kiss your sister?" asked Cozwald.

"I'm a prince, too," Beldegard said, sounding indignant. "But I wouldn't feel right kissing a girl who might not want me to, considering what I look like now. I think he should have a chance instead." Swinging his great head around, he shoved Liam toward the bed. "You're a prince, aren't you? Go ahead. Kiss her."

"I really don't think . . . ," Liam began, but then he glanced at Annie's face and he nodded. "If it's what Annie needs to bring her family back, I'd be happy to help."

"Are you sure?" asked Annie.

"If I don't, we'll always wonder, won't we?"

Beldegard rose up on his hind legs to better see Gwendolyn. "She sure is pretty," he said, and sank down on all fours with an *oof*.

"You know this doesn't change how I feel about you?" Liam said to Annie. "I love you and I always will." Then, before she could respond, he bent down and gave her sister a quick kiss on the lips.

Annie held her breath. She desperately wanted her sister to wake, but not now, not with a kiss from this man!

"I'm so sorry, Annie," Liam said, stepping away from the bed.

At first Annie didn't know why he was apologizing, but when Gwennie didn't move, she realized that it really was over. Nothing had worked. Nothing was going to bring her family back to her. Annie stepped to the side of the bed and gazed down at the flawless alabaster skin of her sister. Tears welled in her eyes as she thought about how her entire family was doomed to sleep for a hundred years. She would find other princes and bring them back here, but if it hadn't worked yet, who was to say that it ever would?

Annie's tears plopped on Gwendolyn's cheek and trickled down as if she herself were crying. Liam rubbed the back of Annie's neck, a small but welcome comfort. She leaned against him. Having someone with her who cared meant so very much.

"What's wrong with her?" the bear prince said, peering

at Gwendolyn. "Is she crying? Nobody should cry in their sleep! Here, let me..." With one big *shlup* of his tongue, Beldegard licked the tears off Gwendolyn's face.

"It's all right," said Annie. "She isn't..."

"Annie, is that you?" Gwendolyn's eyelids fluttered. Beldegard's head was still only inches from hers when she opened her eyes. Her shrill shriek broke the silence of the castle. The sleepers stirred as if dreaming, but no one else came fully awake.

"Gwennie?" said Annie. "You woke up! Is it possible that Beldegard's kiss was enough?"

"If you can call that a kiss," said Liam.

Color flooded Gwendolyn's cheeks as she tried to squirm across the bed and away from the looming bear's head. "Get that beast away from me!" she shouted as Beldegard watched her with soulful eyes.

"He's not a beast!" said Annie. "He's your true love. Beldegard is the one who woke you with a kiss. Don't you see, Gwennie, he's an enchanted prince. His kiss wouldn't have worked if he was just a bear."

"But he's so hairy!" said her sister.

"Give me a minute and I'll prove it to you," Annie said, and moved past Liam to lay her hand on the bear prince's head. Gwendolyn watched, fascinated, as the bear's features slowly melted away into those of a handsome young man.

"His name is Beldegard. He's heir to the throne of the kingdom of Montrose."

"An evil dwarf who wanted my treasure turned me into a bear. I'll remain a bear as long as the dwarf lives. I've been looking for him everywhere and—"

"Sorry to interrupt, but there's something we have to do," said Liam as he used his free hand to reach into his knapsack and pull out a glass bottle. "I don't have a cup, so you're going to have to drink right out of the bottle."

"Is this really the best time?" Gwendolyn asked, looking from Liam to her sister. "Who is he, anyway?" she asked, gesturing to Liam. "He looks familiar."

"He's Prince Liam," said Annie. "He used to work here as a guard. Never mind. I'll explain it all to you later. It's a very long story. Right now you have to drink this or you'll fall asleep again and stay that way for a hundred years."

Gwendolyn shuddered and reached for the bottle. "We wouldn't want that, now would we?" She took a long drink and handed the bottle to Beldegard. "Your turn," she said, even as she managed to look shy.

"Does he need to drink, too?" Liam asked Annie.

"I don't think it would hurt," she said, and shrugged.

A soft breeze lifted the tendrils of hair that curled around Annie's face. The sound of tinkling wind chimes that had been constant since the curse took hold stopped suddenly, making her look up. She noticed that the air looked brighter and no longer smelled stale. Sleepy voices spoke in the next room. Someone laughed in the hallway and a great weight lifted from Annie's heart. Everyone was waking up. Her family was going to be all right.

"I thought I heard you in here," her mother said from the doorway. "How are my girls?"

"We're fine, Mother!" Gwendolyn called out. "Come meet the love of my life. His name is Beldegard and he's an enchanted prince."

"Really?" said the queen as she entered the room. "I'd love to meet him, but first I have to thank Annabelle. Believe it or not, I do remember talking to you while everyone slept," she told Annie. "I don't know how you ended up with this young man instead of Digby, but I'm grateful that you found the right one. Thank you, my darling." And then the queen did something that she hadn't done since the day the fairy Moonbeam cast her spell. She hugged her daughter Annabelle.

"Pardon me," said Prince Cozwald, "but I think it's time we were going."

"And who, pray tell, are you?" asked the queen, turning to face the princes.

"They're the other candidates who were kind enough to try to help us," said Annie.

"Then you are all invited to stay and help us celebrate our awakening. Ah, there's Digby. It's too bad it didn't work out for you and Gwendolyn."

"It's your loss," Digby said. "I'm going home. By your

251

leave, Your Majesty." Turning abruptly, Digby stomped out the door.

"Where's Clarence?" Annie asked, looking around the room.

"He must have left already," said Liam. "Don't worry, there's not much he can do now."

"Mother," Gwendolyn said. "This is Beldegard. I promised him that I would help him find the nasty dwarf who stole his treasure."

"He'll have all the resources of our kingdom to help him, my dear," said the queen. "After all, he is my future son-in-law."

"We need to talk," Liam said, taking Annie by the arm.

Annie nodded, then turned to her mother and bowed. "May we have your leave to go?"

"Of course, my dear," the queen replied, smiling at her younger daughter. "Now Gwendolyn, we should start planning your wedding right away."

Annie wasn't thinking about the bear prince when she left the room, but she knew when he turned back into a bear because she heard her mother cry out, "Oh my, Gwendolyn, your Beldegard really is an enchanted prince!"

Liam's eyes were dancing when he leaned down to Annie and said, "Should we get out of here before they can call you back?"

"Yes, please!" said Annie, and they dashed through

the hall, smiling and waving at all the people who tried to stop them to talk. They didn't slow down until they were in the courtyard, where Captain Sterling was overseeing the guards stripping the remains of the now-withered roses from the portcullis. A fire had been built to burn the thorny rosebushes in the middle of the courtyard, and the flames were already high. Because the heavy iron gate couldn't be lowered until the roses were removed, half a dozen guards were keeping watch as well.

"Excuse me," Liam told Annie, "the captain is here. I should tell him what's been going on."

Annie watched as he crossed the courtyard to the drawbridge. In her eyes Liam was the handsomest man she'd ever known, even handsomer than any prince made so by magic. She loved the way his entire face lit up when he looked at her and the sound of his voice when he said her name. She loved the warmth of his hand when he held hers and the strength of his arms when he'd helped her down from the tower or off the back of a horse. Liam was everything she thought she'd never have and would see only from a distance.

Annie sighed. Here she was, being as silly as Gwendolyn had been when she mooned over Digby. Liam was still talking to the captain when Annie gathered her skirts in her hands and climbed the stairs to the parapet. Watching the bustle of the courtyard was something she had thought about for days and she couldn't wait to do it now. She had reached the top and was turning to wave to Liam when movement in the woods closest to the castle caught her eye. A group of people was coming out of the forest leading a wagon. It was so much like the last time she stood watching a wagon approach the castle from the woods that she wasn't surprised to see it was the same one with the very same markings.

"Liam!" she called over her shoulder. "I think you should see this. Captain Sterling, if you would kindly join me up here as well?"

An old woman was driving the wagon. A cloth had been thrown over the back, covering the cart's contents. Although the men who accompanied the cart were dressed like ordinary farmers, they carried themselves with the straight backs and precise movements of soldiers.

"What is it?" Liam asked as he arrived at the top of the stairs.

"The cart that brought the jeweled spinning wheel is back. If I'm not mistaken, those are some of your father's soldiers."

"My mother's, not my father's," said Liam. "I recognize two of the men who work for her. The woman on the cart is a witch she employs now and then. She's the sister of the one who turned herself into a beetle. They were the only two witches in Dorinocco."

"Which gives her a personal reason not to like us," said Annie.

"There's that, plus I'm sure my mother is paying her a healthy sum."

"I wonder what's in that wagon," Captain Sterling said. "You, Clifton," the captain called down to one of his men in the courtyard. "Call the men to arms and close those drawbridges!" When the soldier saluted and ran off, the captain turned back to the forest and said, "Look, they're taking off the cover. Now we'll know what they've brought us."

As the men removed the cloth, the witch hopped down and turned to face the back of the wagon. Shouting a lot of words that sounded like nonsense to Annie, the old woman twitched her elbows and wiggled her hands, then lifted her arms in the air and twiddled her fingers over the wagon bed. A figure sat up in the bed, its movements slow and jerky. It was crawling down from the wagon when another figure sat up. Soon there were nine figures standing in front of the witch.

"Are those people?" asked Annie, peering at the figures.

Liam shook his head. "If I'm not mistaken, those are statues. I carved them myself years ago. I made them as a gift for my father."

"I remember them!" said Annie. "They were standing against the walls in your Great Hall."

"You can do magic?" asked Captain Sterling.

"Not at all," Liam replied. "They were ordinary wooden statues when I made them. That witch is the one making them move. Look, she's sending them this way."

Captain Sterling looked puzzled. "What does she think she's going to do with a bunch of statues?"

"I don't know, but I don't like it," said Liam.

The soldiers were armed now and handing weapons to the statues. With the soldiers ranked on either side, the statues began a ragged march to the castle walls.

"I told you to get that drawbridge closed!" the captain shouted to the men below. Metal clanged for a moment, then stopped abruptly.

"We can't, Captain!" shouted one of his men. "The gears are still jammed with roses!"

"I hate it when magic gums up the works," said the captain. "You there," he shouted to the approaching soldiers. "What is your purpose in coming here?"

"I think you know that already," said one of the soldiers who had kept to the back. He strode forward now and Annie could see that it was Clarence wearing farmer's clothes.

"I should have known he wouldn't give up," said Liam. "Let me go talk to him and … There, in that trench! They have archers. Duck!" he shouted as arrows shot from a trench alongside the road leading from the woods. The arrows rose high into the sky, then plummeted down, hitting the stone courtyard with the clatter of breaking wood.

"They must have dug that trench while everyone was asleep," said the captain, crouching down beside the princess. "Stay down, Your Highness," he said, and took a quick peek over the edge of the parapet. "They're heading for the gate. Return fire!" he ordered.

Annie looked up as arrows arched overhead, landing in the trench and the ground around it. Some of the arrows hit the statues, but all they did was knock a few of the marching figures off their stride or chip a piece from a wooden shoulder.

"You stay here, Your Highness," said the captain as he started down the stairs.

"I'm coming with you," Liam announced, taking two steps at a time.

Annie tried to do what Captain Sterling had said, but when she heard fighting below her in the courtyard, she couldn't wait any longer. Creeping to the edge of the walkway, she saw Clarence standing to the side, watching as soldiers fought soldiers while others grappled with the wooden statues. Although her father's soldiers hacked at the statues with axes, their blades did little damage. The statues moved slowly and were easily avoided, but the strength of their wooden arms was twice that of ordinary men.

There was a roar and the fighting shifted as Clarence's

men forced her father's soldiers back to the door of the castle keep. Liam and Captain Sterling fought valiantly side by side, but even they were no match for the statues who blocked their way at every turn.

Annie gasped when she saw Liam barely escape being run through with a statue's sword. "That's enough of that!" she muttered as she slipped down the stairs. "Maybe they can't do anything about those statues, but I can."

While the fighting raged at one end of the courtyard, Annie drew as close to the fray as she could manage and waited for her chance. As soon as one of the statues at the edge of the fighting stood with its back to her, Annie darted forward and touched it. The magic went out of the statue in an instant, and it fell to the ground with a *thunk*. The statue was heavy and it took all of Annie's strength to drag it across the courtyard to the fire still burning in the middle. She was dragging her second statue when Clarence saw what she was doing.

"Get the girl!" he shouted, but Liam was there before him, protecting Annie with a sword in one hand and an ax in the other. With Captain Sterling leading them, her father's soldiers flocked to her, adding their weapons to Liam's.

Annie ran to touch another statue, but this time the witch saw her. The old woman was taller than the witch Annie had met in the tower, and looked just as mean.

"I've heard about you," said the witch. "You're the one who takes away magic. Well, you won't get mine!"

"Then you should leave now or I'll take your magic just like I took theirs!" Annie said, pointing to the smoldering sticks that were the last remains of the two statues.

"You won't have to," the witch snarled. "Because I'm going to give it to you!" Raising her hands above her head, the witch did a little dance, hopping from one foot to the other while shouting words Annie had never heard before. The magic grated on Annie's ears, sounding harsh and tinny. A cloud of muddy green light formed between the witch's hands, getting bigger the longer she danced. Suddenly the witch stopped and thrust her hands at Annie. The cloud drifted toward her, settling around her like a fog around the castle. Annie could still hear the magic, but she didn't feel anything at all, even when the cloud began to seethe and pop. She watched as it sloughed off her, dripping like thick molasses onto the ground.

"What did you do?" demanded the witch.

The sound of the magic changed, becoming faster, more insistent. The green glow rose from a near puddle on the ground, re-forming as a cloud in the air between Annie and the witch. And then, in less time than it takes to blink, the cloud hurtled at the witch, covering her from head to toe. The old woman screeched as her body began to jerk, and she fell over, a wooden statue identical to the others. Annie looked around as the other statues fell, lifeless.

Clarence had come closer to watch what happened to Annie. Seeing the witch fall instead was more than he could take. "Retreat!" he shouted, running for the drawbridge. The sound of running feet hitting stone filled the courtyard as his men tore after him.

"Captain!" shouted one of the Treecrest soldiers. "I think we can close this drawbridge now."

"Then do it!" yelled Captain Sterling.

Liam came to stand beside Annie as the drawbridge began to rise. They watched as the last of Clarence's men scrabbled over the top only moments before it closed.

"When I told you that most of the fairies stayed away from my christening, I didn't mention the few who did come bringing simple gifts," said Liam. "I can whistle any tune, whittle just about anything, and I have very attractive feet."

Annie smiled. "You don't say? And do any of these things change when I'm around?"

"Of course. When you're nearby I can't whistle a tune, my whittling is pathetic, and my shoes get tight."

"Oh dear!"

"It's sad, but true. However, I can do without any of

these things as long as I don't have to do without one thing."

"Oh really?" said Annie. "And what might that be?"

"You," he said, pulling her into his arms.

ACKNOWLEDGMENTS

I would like to thank Ellie, who has a wonderful sense of humor; Kim, my horse expert and mapmaker; and Victoria, who has taught me so much about writing that I often know the answer when I wonder, What would Victoria say?